Library of
Davidson College

A Garland Series

The Flowering of the Novel

Representative Mid-Eighteenth Century Fiction 1740-1775

A Collection of 121 Titles

The Lives of
Cleopatra and Octavia

Sarah Fielding

Garland Publishing, Inc., New York & London

1974

Copyright © 1974
by Garland Publishing, Inc.
All Rights Reserved

Bibliographical note:

this facsimile was made from a copy in the
Library of the University of Illinois
(x823.F465l.1757)

Library of Congress Cataloging in Publication Data

Fielding, Sarah, 1710-1768.
  The lives of Cleopatra and Octavia.

  (The Flowering of the novel)
  Reprint of the 1757 ed. printed for the author,
and sold by A. Millar, London.
  1. Cleopatra, Queen of Egypt, d. 30 B.C.--Fiction.
2. Octavia, wife of Mark Antony, d. B.C. 11--Fiction.
I. Title. II. Series.
PZ3.F4604Li6 [PR3459.F3]   823'.5   74-17294
ISBN 0-8240-1147-3

Printed in the United States of America

TO THE

Countess of *POMFRET*.

MADAM,

HE Lives of *Cleopatra* and *Octavia* form, perhaps, the strongest Contrast of any Ladies celebrated in History.

Cleopatra presents us with the abandoned Consequences, and the fatal Catastrophe, of an haughty, false, and intriguing Woman; whose only Views were to exert her Charms, and prostitute her Power, to the Gratification of a boundless Vanity and Avarice, without Regard to the Ruin of her Country, or the Sufferings of others.

The amiable and gentle *Octavia* gives us, on the reverse, an Example of all those Graces and Embellishments,

Dedication.

bellishments worthy the moſt refined Female Character. The Dignity ſhe preſerved, and the Delicacy of her Manners, became her elevated Station, and were an Ornament to the politeſt Court. She patronized the Learned, and was of a truly *Roman* Spirit, in ſacrificing her private to the public Good. Nor did this Heroine ſhine with leſs Luſtre in perſonal than in public Virtues. She was a ſincere Friend, an affectionate Siſter, a faithful Wife, and both a tender and inſtructive Parent. Such was the accompliſhed Character of *Octavia!*

These are the Two different Pictures I have endeavoured to repreſent; and if I have been ſo happy as to draw them in any manner to afford your Ladyſhip the leaſt Pleaſure in the Peruſal, and not to diſgrace the Honour of your Patronage, my Pains will be amply compenſated. I am,

Madam,

With great Reſpect,

Your Ladyſhip's moſt Obliged,

and Obedient Humble Servant,

S. Fielding.

A LIST

OF THE

SUBSCRIBERS.

A.

THE Right Honourable Lady Arundel
Lord Anson
Lady Anson
Lady Allen   2 Books
William Adams, *Esq*;   2 Books
Mrs. Adams   2 Books
Ralph Allen, *Esq*;   2 Books
Mrs. Allen   2 Books
Michael Adolphus, *Esq*;
John Gay Alleyne, *Esq*;
Edward Aftly, *Esq*;
George Abercrombie, *Esq*;
Mrs. Acton
Christopher Arnold, *Esq*;
Doctor Armstrong
George Anfren, *Esq*;
Mrs. Alexander

B.

The Duke *of* Beaufort
The Duchess *of* Beaufort
The Earl *of* Bath
Lord Boyd
Sir William Bunbury, *Bart.*
The Countess *of* Barrymore   16 Books
The Hon. Mr. Hamilton Boyle
Lady Jane Bridges
Sir Wiiliam Boothby, *Bart.*
Mrs. Boothby Skrymsher
Cha. Boothby Skrymsher, *Esq*;
Mr. Burk
Charles Bohun, *Esq*;
—— Bluett, *Esq*;
Mrs. Beckford
Mrs. Burkit
Mrs. Ball

A List of the Subscribers.

Mrs. Busby
Miss Bayne
Mrs. Brotherton
William Barnard, *Esq*;
Ballard Beckford, *Esq*;
Doctor Brewster
John Brathwaite, *Esq*;
Henry Brounker, *Esq*;
William Bateman, *Esq*;
Pusey Brooke, *Esq*;
The Rev. Doctor Best   2 *Books*
Mrs. Best
Mrs. Bury
—— Barlow, *Esq*;
The Rev. Mr. Bailey
Mrs. Bailey
Mr. Busby
James Mag. Batten, *Esq*;
Mr. Berkin
Mr. Bayne
Francis Barrel, *Esq*;
Thomas Bush, *Esq*;
—— Burke, *Esq*;
Thomas Bohun, *Esq*;
Miss Blackbourne
Richard Backwell, *Esq*;
—— Barratt, *Esq*;
Edward Benson, *Esq*;   2 *Books*
—— Bennet, *Esq*;
Mrs. Barker   2 *Books*
Miss Barker
Colonel Burton   2 *Books*
Mrs. Baker
The Rev. Mr. Sackville Spencer Bale
Mr. Bourke
—— Berenger, *Esq*;
—— Barrell, *Esq*;

—— Blackbourne, *Esq*;
—— Burrows, *Esq*;   2 *Books*
Miss Burrows
Miss Amy Burrows
Miss Betty Burrows
The Rev. Mr. Barford

C.

The Earl of Chesterfield   3 *Books*
The Right Honourable the Lady Anne, *Countess of* Coventry
Lady Mary Coke
Lady Anne Connolly   2 *Books*
Lady Cox
Rev. Doctor Clarke, *Dean of* Salisbury
Rev. Doctor Creswick, *Dean of* Wells
The Earl of Clanricarde
Mrs. Elizabeth Cutts
Doctor Carlton
Miss Anne Calvert
Sir John Cope
Colonel Mure Campbell
William Collier, *Esq*;
Robert Carey, *Esq*;
James Cooke, *Esq*;
Mrs. Crawford
Honourable Mrs. Cavendish
Thomas Cooper, *Esq*;
Richard Cox, *Esq*;
Mrs. Craiesteyne
Samuel Cox, *Esq*;
Saville Cockayne Cust, *Esq*;
Mr. Cockbourne
Mr. Benjamin Cockbourne
Mrs. Cavendish

Captain

A List of the Subscribers.

Captain Cunningham
Mrs. Channing
Mrs. Cotes
John Calvert, *Esq;*
Colonel Clayton
Captain Clements
Lady Codrington
Richard Champion, *Esq;*
William Champion, *Esq;*
—— Cutts, *Esq;* 2 *Books*
John Catanach, *Esq;*
The Rev. Mr. Cawthorn
Miss Cocke
Miss Carr
Awnsham Churchill, *Esq;*
Miss Mary Calvert
—— Chetwynde, *Esq;*
—— Champion, *Esq;*
Mr. Clutterbuck
Mr. Crank
Miss Cornwall

D.

The Countess of Denbigh
The Countess of Dysart
The Countess of Dalkeith
Lady Anne Dawson   6 *Books*
The Rev. Doctor Delany, *Dean of* Down   10 *Books*
—— Dawson, *sen. Esq;* 6 *Books*
—— Dawson, *jun. Esq;* 6 *Books*
Gibson Dalzell, *Esq;*
—— Deval, *Esq;*
Lord Digby
William Duncombe, *Esq;*
Miss Dean
Miss Davies
Miss Devie

Mr. Dodsley   6 *Books*

E.

The Countess of Essex
Lady Charlotte Edwin 2 *Books*
Lady Sophia Egerton
Miss Edwin
John Eaton, *Esq;*
William Earle, *Esq;*
Henry Earle, *Esq;*
The Rev. Mr. Exton
—— Exeter, *Esq;*
Mrs. Exeter

F.

Lady Augustus Fitzroy
Lady Caroline Fox
Lady Mary Fitzgerald
Governor Fleming   4 *Books*
Francis Fane, *Esq;*
James Frampton, *Esq;*
Cope Freeman, *Esq;*
—— Frazer, *Esq;*
The Rev. Mr. Thomas Franklyn
The Rev. Mr. Thomas Frankland
—— Fell, *Esq;*
—— Fairfax, *Esq;*
Mr. Thomas Freeman
—— Fitz-Patrick, *Esq;*

G.

The Marquis of Granby
The Hon. Henry Grenville
The Hon. Mrs. Grenville
Fulke Greville, *Esq;*
Mrs. Greville

A List of the Subscribers.

The Rev. Doctor Garnett
Doctor Garnier
Colonel Griffin
Doctor Glym
John Gray, *Esq*;　　2 *Books*
Henry Gould, *Esq*;　2 *Books*
The Rev. Mr. Gould　2 *Books*
Miss Gould　　　　　2 *Books*
Miss Jane Gould　　 2 *Books*
Thomas Gould, *Esq*; 2 *Books*
David Garrick, *Esq*;
Edward Gwatkin, *Esq*;
Edward Goofe, *Esq*;
Mrs. Gregor
Mrs. Anna Grove
Thomas Gore, *Esq*;
Mrs. Gore
Mrs. Graham
Miss Goodall
Mrs. Griffith
Mrs. Gregory
Mr. George Goldfinch

H.
The Countess of Harcourt
The Countess of Harrington
The Hon. Mrs. Hamilton
Sir Charles Howard　2 *Books*
Colonel Honeywood　 2 *Books*
Sir Thomas Harrison
Colonel Howard
Lady Hickman
Rev. Mr. Chancellor Hoadly 2 *Books*
Doctor Hoadly
Doctor Haye
James Harris, *Esq*;

Thomas Harris, *Esq*;
The Rev. Mr. Harris
Mrs. Harris
Charles Hedges, *Esq*;
George Hunt, *Esq*;
Mrs. Hill
Henry Hoare, *Esq*;
Mrs. Hoare
Stephen Holland, *Esq*;
Mrs. Hamilton
Mrs. Harrington
Miss Holford
Henry Harris, *Esq*;
Mrs. Harris
Mrs. Hussey
Gabriel Hanger, *Esq*;
Counsellor Hussey
Banks Hodgkinson, *Esq*;
William Hedges, *Esq*;
Mrs. Henshaw
Mrs. Hume
John Hide, *Esq*;　　2 *Books*
John Young Husband, *Esq*;
Charles Hedges, *jun*. *Esq*;
John Hughs, *Esq*;
Charles Hamilton, *Esq*;
Miss Hall
Miss Highmore
The Rev. Mr. Hanmer
Mrs. Hodgson
Mrs. Horton
Mr. Hughs
Mr. Hogarth

I.
The Countess of Jersey
Doctor Jacob

Doctor

A List of the Subscribers.

Doctor Jennings
Colonel Jessop
The Rev. Mr. Canon Jenkins
Mrs. Elizabeth Ifted
Mrs. Jeffreys
Mrs. Jones
Mrs. Jennings
The Rev. Mr. Jackson

K.
The Countess of Kildare
The Hon. and Rev. Mr. Keppel
James Kearney, *Esq*;
Captain Killegrew
Mrs. Killegrew
Mrs. Knight
The Rev. Mr. King
Mr. Kittoe

L.
The Earl of Loudoun
Lord Lyttleton   2 *Books*
The Bishop of Londonderry
The Hon. Mr. James Lumley
The Hon. Mr. Leeson
Doctor Lucas
Walter Long, *Esq*;
Richard Luther, *Esq*;
Luke Lilingston, *Esq*;
—— Langlois, *Esq*;
Herbert Lloyd, *Esq*;
Mrs. Julia Leslie
Mr. Lovell
Stephen Lebas *Esq*;
Mr. Langford

M.
The Duchess of Marlborough   2 *Books*
The Countess of Middlesex
Lady Barbara Mountagu
Lady Viscountess Molesworth
Mrs. Mountagu
Edward Wortley Mountague, *Esq*;   10 *Books*
Wortley Mountague, *jun. Esq*;
Humphry Morrice, *Esq*;
Moses Mendez Da Costa, *Esq*;
Henry Morley, *Esq*;
Mrs. Maccartney
Mr. Mordett
Doctor Mabb
Miss Meynell
Mrs. Morton
—— Martin, *Esq*;
—— Mendez, *Esq*;
Mr. Millar   6 *Books*
Miss Mitchell

N.
The Earl of Northumberland
The Countess of Northumberland
Lord Viscount Newnham
Mrs. Naylor
Colonel Nugent
Mrs. Neale
Richard Nash, *Esq*;
Mr. Joseph Nichols

O.
Sir William Owen, *Bart.*
Doctor Oliver

A List *of the* Subscribers.

Mrs. Owen
Miss Otteley
—— Oflarty, *Esq*; 2 *Books*

P.
The Earl of Powis
The Countess of Powis
Lady Beauchamp Proctor
Jonath. Moreton Pleydell, *Esq*;
John Preston, *Esq*;
Richard Parrot, *Esq*;
William Pagett, *Esq*;
Uvedale Price, *Esq*;
Miss Palmer
Miss Pinke
Constantine Phipps, *Esq*;
Thomas Potter, *Esq*;
Mr. Jerry Peirce
Miss Percival
Miss Palmer
—— Paterson, *Esq*;
Richard Pottenger, *Esq*;
John Philipson, *Esq*;
Christopher Perry, *Esq*;

R.
Mrs. Rooke
George Rice, *Esq*;
Morrice Robinson, *Esq*;
Mrs. Robinson
Henry Reade, *Esq*;
John Reade, *Esq*;
Mr. Richardson   4 *Books*
Mrs. Richardson   2 *Books*
A Gentleman, through the Hands of Mr. R.   10 *Books*
Mrs. Robinson

Mr. Reynell
Mr. Robinson
Mr. Riggs
Mrs. Ravaud
Mr. Roberts

S.
The Duke of Somerset
The Earl of Stamford   2 *Books*
The Countess of Shaftesbury
The Earl of Strafford
The Countess of Strafford
The Countess of Shelburn
Lord Southwell
Lady Southwell   2 *Books*
Lady Jane Stanhope
Lady Catherine Stanhope
The Hon. Mrs. Spencer
Charles Stanhope, *Esq*; 2 *Books*
Doctor Smallbrooke
Augustus Schutz, *Esq*;
George Scott, *Esq*;
William Sharpe, *Esq*;
Mrs. Sawyer
Mr. Saunderson
Mrs. Shornicrofs
Miss Stevens
—— Sheldon, *Esq*;
The Rev. Mr. Smith
Mr. Simpson
Mr. Sumner
John Strange, *Esq*;
Mrs. Scott
Mr. Sharp
John Scrimshire, *Esq*;
Miss Scrimshire
—— Sharp, *Esq*;

Walter

A List of the Subscribers.

Walter Strickland, *Esq*;
Mrs. Sloper
Mrs. Swymmer
Coulston Stow, *Esq*;
John Sergent, *Esq*;
Mrs. E. Scott
Doctor Shomberg
——— Sloper, *Esq*;
The Rev. Mr. Sanderson
Captain Stephens
——— Smith, *Esq*;
The Rev. Mr. Skynner
Mr. Stanly

T.

The Earl of Tankerville
The Earl of Tilney
Lady Viscountess Teynham
Lord Talbot
Sir Robert Throgmorton, *Bart.*
Thomas Tash, *Esq*;
Mrs. Tash
Joseph Tully, *Esq*;
Mr. Taylor
James Tooker, *Esq*;
Thomas Towers, *Esq*; 20 *Books*
Captain Tucker
Mrs. Towers
Mrs. Tower
Mrs. Foster Tuffnell
John Trenchard, *Esq*;
——— Tomlinson, *Esq*;
Miss Talbot
Mrs. Tudway
Mrs. Thornton
Alexander Thistlethwaite, *Esq*;
Richard Trevor, *Esq*;

Miss Temple

U.

Lord Viscount Villiers
Lady Harriot Vernon
Mrs. Upton
Wilmot Vaughan, *Esq*;

W.

Lord Viscount Windsor 10 *Books*
Lady Frances Williams 2 *Books*
The Hon. Mrs. Wadman
The Hon. Mrs. Wilmot
The Hon. Mr. Wesly
The Rev. Mr. Canon Walker
The Rev. Mr. Canon Wheeler
William Wyndham, *Esq*;
Richard Willis, *Esq*;
William Wilson, *Esq*;
John Wadman, *Esq*;
Thomas Walters, *Esq*;
Wadham Windham, *Esq*;
George James Williams, *Esq*;
Miss Ward
Thomas Worsley, *Esq*;
Mrs. Warburton
Thomas Wood, *Esq*;
Mrs. Wood
Thomas Walker, *Esq*;.
Mr. Walker
Mrs. Worsley
Thomas Wallis, *Esq*;
The Rev. Mr. Walsh
William Whitehead, *Esq*; 2 *Books*
The Rev. Mr. Thomas Walker
The Rev. Mr. Wetstein

John

A List of the Subscribers.

John Wilks, *Esq*;
Mr. Watson   2 *Books*
The Rev. Mr. Wright
John Rolle Walter, *Esq*;
Mrs. Woolaston
Edward Weston, *Esq*;

Richard Warner, *Esq*;
Saunders Welch, *Esq*; 10 *Books*
Mr. Henry Woodward

Y.

John Yates, *Esq*;

THE LIVES

OF

CLEOPATRA

AND

OCTAVIA.

BY

The AUTHOR of DAVID SIMPLE.

LONDON:

Printed for the AUTHOR,
And Sold by ANDREW MILLAR, in the *Strand*;
R. and J. DODSLEY, in *Pall-Mall*;
and J. LEAKE, at *Bath*.
M.DCC.LVII.

INTRODUCTION.

FEW Parts of Writing afford the Mind a more grateful Variety, enrich it with more copious Inftruction, or more engagingly tempt it to look into, and know itfelf, than Biography; or the Lives of Perfons whofe fuperior Talents, Power, and Station; or whofe uncommon Turns of Fortune, have diverfified their Characters, and diftinguifhed them from the reft of our Species.

The Soul, fond of Entertainment, is hence furnifhed with a fumptuous Feaft; which, if ferved up with Elegance, and mixed with Attic Salt, feldom difgufts the Palate, or offends the Appetite----The Gueft rifes chearful, and departs in good Humour; well pleafed with his Fare, and the Author's Invitation.

INTRODUCTION.

The Reader, like a Traveller, herein views the Manners of human Nature, and Customs of the World; the Intrigues of Policy, the Arts of Lovers, and the Exploits of Heroes; with the secret Springs and Motives of their Actions, at a much easier Expence indeed, and with no more Labour than turning over a new Leaf; which often unfolds to him as unexpected a Scene, and different a Prospect, as if he had changed his Climate, or taken a Flight from one Region to another.

For such Reasons the celebrated *Montaigne* recommends the Lives of *Plutarch*, as the most useful and valuable Treasure of antient Learning. And it is perhaps from his happy Manner of intermixing the Circumstances of his own Life, we derive not a little of the Satisfaction we have in the Perusal of that ingenious and amusing Author himself.

From the same Taste of being acquainted with the various and surprising Incidents of Mankind, arises our insatiable Curiosity for Novels or Romances: Infatuated with a Sort of Knight errantry, we draw these fictitious Characters into a real Existence; and thus, pleasingly deluded, we find ourselves as warmly interested, and deeply affected by the imaginary Scenes
of

INTRODUCTION.

of *Arcadia*, the wonderful Atchievements of Don *Quixote*, the merry Conceits of *Sancho*, rural Innocence of a *Joseph Andrews*, or the inimitable Virtues of Sir *Charles Grandison*, as if they were real, and those romantic Heroes had experienced the capricious Fortunes attributed to them by the fertile Invention of the Writers.

Performances of this Kind have indeed one Advantage; that, as they are the Works of Fancy, the Author, like a Painter, may so colour, decorate, and embellish them, as most agreeably flatter our Humour, and most highly promise to entertain, captivate, and enchant the Mind.

But to balance this, it may be offered in Recommendation of the Lives of Persons who have really made their Appearance on the Stage of the World, that their Actions are better suited to inform, and give us juster Notions of ourselves, as they are Originals, and present the Eye with the Prospect of human Nature, taken from Life, and not extended beyond the Limits of Credibility and Truth. The one, like false Coin, is rather calculated to deceive, than profit us; whilst the other, like current Gold, is of intrinsic Value, and may, with greater Certainty, be disposed of, or applied to our Service and Emolument.

Thus the famous Amours of *Anthony* and *Cleopatra*, having a true Foundation, will more effectually impress the fatal Consequences of a mad intoxicated Lover, and a false insinuating Woman, than may be expected from the most admired or accomplished Novels; and the Distresses of a virtuous *Octavia* will excite a more lasting Sensibility of Pity or Relentment, than can be indulged from the most pathetic Descriptions of Romance. For in the latter the Reader seldom so far forgets himself, as not to recollect that the Characters are imaginary and feigned; whereas the former, like true Mirrours, reflect the real Images of our Persons.

These superior Advantages of real Characters induced the Author of the Lives of *Cleopatra* and *Octavia* to select the most interesting Parts of their Histories for the Entertainment of the Public. But as the modern Relish for Works of Imagination would almost tempt her to despair of Approbation, without some Mixture of Romance, she has, in Complaisance to this Taste, introduced the Lives of those Ladies, as supposed to have been delivered by them-

INTRODUCTION.

themselves in the Shades below. By which Method the Reader may at least expect a more impartial, distinct, and exact Narrative of their several Adventures, and of the Motives they were influenced by; unless he is so inveterately prejudiced in Disfavour of the Fair-sex, as to presume, with the ill-natured Satyrist, That a Woman is not to be credited, any more than trusted, tho' dead.

The Author begs Leave to account for her Interview with those Heroines, as *Homer*, *Virgil*, *Aristophanes*, *Lucan*, and others, have on the like Occasion, through the Assistance of an Eastern Sorcerer or Magician, who conveyed her to the gloomy Realms of *Pluto*, and by his Interest at Court, prevailed on that grand Monarch to command those celebrated Shades to give her a faithful Detail of their Lives, during their Abode on Earth. There was no disputing his Orders; and the only Shadow the imperious Queen of *Egypt* retained of her former Royalty, was, the Permission granted her to take Place of *Octavia*, in the Recital of her Story, which she did in the following Manner.

THE
LIFE
OF
CLEOPATRA.

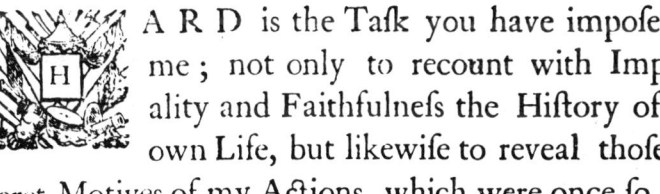ARD is the Task you have imposed on me; not only to recount with Impartiality and Faithfulness the History of my own Life, but likewise to reveal those secret Motives of my Actions, which were once so little known to myself, that I was almost as much the Object of my own Deceit, as were either of my powerful Lovers. The Knowlege of these Motives is not to be attained without the deepest Reflection.----Indeed, the first Impulse of the human Mind is frequently so very foreign to the Action it afterwards produces,

produces, and so very unlike the Colours wherein we represent that Action to ourselves, that it is often impossible for us, by any Reflection, to be acquainted with all the Secrets of our Souls, whilst imprisoned in the Body, and blinded by Passion. However, I am at present possessed of this Knowlege, and shall obey your irresistible Command, in giving you a true Picture of myself; and happy is it, that I am now divested of Vanity, since I shall here have so little Opportunity to flatter and gratify that insatiable Passion.

Nothing remarkable passed in my Infancy; only as I was born a Princess, my Father being King of *Egypt*, the Respect and Distance with which I was treated, instilled very early into my Mind the Notion, that to please myself was the sole Business of my Life, and that every one around me was born to be my Slave.

I had two Brothers, and a Sister; but being myself the Eldest, and my Father entertaining an apparent Prejudice in my Favour, I used these with all the Insolence the high Conceit of my Merit could dictate or suggest.

CLEOPATRA.

In short, as I was naturally of a Disposition so selfish as to direct every Person, and to center every Desire within the narrow Compass of my own Gratification; and as this Talent was likewise improved by Education, my elevated Fancy (even whilst I was yet very young) looked upon the rest of Mankind with the utmost Contempt; and I considered them as no more capable of Feeling, than if they were inanimate.---The Pleasures or Pains of others were to me of so little Importance, that I lived as if I had been the only Creature on Earth who had any Sensation. And yet, had Mankind been so unsusceptible of Pleasure or Pain, how should I have been disappointed in pursuing my Revenge on those who in any manner piqued my Pride, in not paying me the Adoration which I thought my Due.

When my Father *Ptolomy Auletes* died, he left his Crown to me and my Brother *Ptolomy Dionysius*, whom, according to the *Egyptian* Custom, I was to marry. But *Pothinus*, *Achillas*, and *Theodotus*, three Men of ambitious Spirits (who wanted to divide between them all the Power and Revenues of the Kingdom) had got my Brother into their Hands. He by their Advice raised such a Force to assist *Pompey* in the civil Wars between him and *Cæsar*, as engaged

engaged *Pompey*, by a Decree of the Senate, to give the Crown of *Egypt* wholly to my Brother. And yet this *Pompey* after the Battle of *Pharsalia*, when he fled to my Brother for Refuge from the Pursuits of *Cæsar*, was murdered on the *Egyptian* Shore by the Intrigues of those very Men, who had advised the levying Troops for his Assistance, and Relief.

I rejoiced in *Pompey*'s Death from that Spirit of Revenge, always predominant in me. For Pride my darling Passion was injured, when any Man presumed to be my Enemy. This is one Example of what I above observed of its being impossible whilst alive, to be apprised of all the Motives of our Actions; since this was a Secret no Reflection could then have acquainted me with. Many other Instances of which will recur in the Sequel of this Relation.

When *Cæsar*, after the Death of *Pompey*, came to *Alexandria*, I, with my Sister *Arsinoe*, was in *Syria* raising Troops in order to recover my Crown. But as soon as I heard the Conqueror was in *Egypt*, I resolved to hasten thither, and plead my own Cause in Person: For I thought the Grace and Beauty of the Pleader would avail more, than the utmost Eloquence

quence another could employ in my Behalf. And indeed it proved agreeable to my Expectation; for *Cæsar*, though he gave Audience to my Agents, yet determined nothing till my Arrival.

Arsinoe, and my younger Brother, obtained an easy Admittance into *Alexandria*; but *Achillas*, my Brother's General, jealous that I was come to claim my Right, which himself, and his Accomplices had usurped, took all possible Precaution to hinder me from seeing *Cæsar*. However, as the Success of this Point depended on Stratagem, they in vain endeavoured to frustrate and prevent it. My Delight in over-reaching others was so great, that putting me on the Invention of Artifice only served to supply an Opportunity of gratifying my natural Disposition, and of exercising my most favourite Talent.

Accompanied therefore by *Apollodorus* the *Sicilian*, I got into a little Skiff, or Galley, and in the Dusk of the Evening landed near the Palace. Although I found it would be very difficult to gain an Interview without Discovery; yet, being resolved to accomplish it, I placed myself on a Feather-bed; which *Apollodorus*, binding up together with the Bedding, carried on his Back, with me therein concealed

cealed, through the Castle Gates into *Cæsar*'s Apartment. *Cæsar*, pleased with the Ingenuity of the Contrivance, and charmed with the Air in which I suddenly started up, and presented myself to his Sight, from that Moment became my Lover.

I shall not here relate the Manner wherein I managed *Cæsar*'s Passion, nor the Arts made use of by me to work and engage him to my Designs, as there will be so much to offer on that Subject in the Account I shall have Occasion to give of my Intrigues with *Mark Anthony*. My Invention, improved by Experience, then shone in its highest Lustre; and therefore, to avoid needless Repetitions, I shall at present only mention such Matters of Fact as are proper for your Information.

Cæsar at first returned me my Crown to the entire Exclusion of my Brother; yet afterwards, in order to appease the *Alexandrians*, he placed him in Partnership with me on the *Egyptian* Throne. *Achillas* being disgusted, his Ambition excited him to raise new Commotions, wherein he had the Address to engage *Ptolomy Dionysius* to conspire with him. However, *Cæsar*, after several Engagements, in a decisive Battle obtained so compleat a Victory, that

that *Ptolomy* was obliged to seek Refuge by Flight; but in endeavouring to gain his Ships on the River *Nile* was drowned in the Attempt.

On this Event *Cæsar* joined my younger Brother, a Prince of eleven Years old, in the royal Dignity with me: And *Cæsar* himself continued my Guest near a Twelvemonth. All this Time we indulged the utmost Profusion of Luxury, that my own, or the Invention of any of my Courtiers could dictate, or the Power of *Cæsar* could execute.

At the Expiration of the Year, a necessary War engaged my Lover to depart. The Separation sat heavy on my Mind, as I looked on the Conquest over *Cæsar*'s Affections to be highly worthy my most assiduous Endeavours to preserve. Fain would I have accompanied him; and such was the tender Fondness he expressed towards me, that he would have gladly consented, had not his Soldiers peremptorily insisted on his leaving me behind. It would be needless to intimate the Good-will I entertained for these Soldiers; tho' it was some Satisfaction to observe that it was *Cæsar*, and not me, they disobeyed. And I was also not a little pleased with their Jealousy
of

of my Power over their Commander, which their Conduct so plainly avowed.

Soon after his Departure I was brought to bed of a Son; whom, in Honour to *Cæsar*, and by his Permission, I called *Cæsarion*.

On his Return to *Rome*, *Cæsar* had my Image placed next to that of *Venus* in the Temple he had built and dedicated to this Goddess of Beauty. As soon as informed of the Adoration he remembered me with I desired Leave to attend him at *Rome*. He granted my Request, and I took my Brother along with me. *Cæsar* allotted me an Apartment in his own Palace, and was so open in his Gallantries, as well as attentive to my Pleasures, that it gave great Offence to the *Romans*; and particularly in respect to *Calphurnia*, his Wife. However, my Triumph over his Heart was so absolute, that no other Motive could have forced him from my Arms, than the Necessity of his Presence in *Spain* to finish the War which then raged in that Country. His Tenderness for me prevailed on him to recommend my going back to *Egypt*; as he thought it extremely improper to venture or expose myself to the Resentment of a

jealous

jealous Wife. I accordingly complied with his Advice, and returned to *Egypt*, loaded with magnificent Prefents.

My Precaution fuggefted to me the Policy of leaving my Brother behind. I was apprehenfive that as he grew older, he would claim his Share in the Government of my Kingdom; and therefore, to prevent this Confequence, I contrived to have him poifoned at *Rome*, where, as he was a Stranger, his Cataftrophe would be better concealed than in *Egypt*.

On my Arrival at *Alexandria*, the firft News I heard, was the Affaffination of *Cæfar* in the Senate by *Brutus*, and his Accomplices. Tears and unavailing Sorrow appeared to me fruitlefs; and therefore all the Refpect I fhewed the Memory of this mighty Hero, was an immediate Engagement with the eldeft Son of his greateft Enemy; namely, *Pompey*. I imagined, now *Cæfar* was no more, that the Family of *Pompey* would in all likelihood flourifh again at *Rome*; and fo that it was my Intereft to cultivate the Friendfhip of the Head of this illuftrious Family.

During

During the civil War between the Murderers of *Cæsar*, and the Avengers of that Murder, it was my Study to keep in Favour with both Parties; for the promoting of which Defign, whilft I difpatched Troops to the Affiftance of *Dolabella* in *Syria*, I commanded *Serapion* my Lieutenant in *Cyprus*, to declare for *Caffius*.

But after the celebrated Battle of *Philippi*, when *Auguftus Cæfar* and *Mark Anthony* were in Fact Mafters of the World (although they allowed the feeble-fpirited *Lepidus* the Name of a Triumvir) *Anthony* came into *Cilicia*, and fent *Dellius* to fummon me to appear in Perfon before him, in order to juftify myfelf from the Accufation of having affifted the Enemies of *Cæfar*.

As foon as *Dellius* had made me acquainted with the Commands of *Anthony*, I was immediately ftruck with the pleafing Thought of the fortunate Opportunity I fhould have of enfnaring the amorous Triumvir by thofe artful Wiles which Experience had fo much improved; and which had long ago been ftrong enough to entangle the great and mighty *Cæfar*.

I asked *Dellius* many Questions concerning *Anthony*, with an Air of anxious Sorrow and particular Concern, lest I should any-ways appear to have offended him. At the same time I also put on a languishing Look, which moved the Compassion of *Dellius*. He, to assuage my Trouble, begged Leave to assure me, that my personal Charms would be an ample Protection against the Resentment of *Anthony*; who, he was very confident, would have far greater Occasion to be apprehensive of the dangerous Tendency of viewing Beauty such as mine.

Cæsar and *Pompey* had indeed already convinced me, that the Power of my own Charms was sufficient to encourage me to give the Words of *Dellius* an easy Credit. From this Moment I looked on *Anthony* as my Prey, and was sure of conquering him. I dismissed *Dellius* with Presents, and humble Messages to his Lord; promising to obey his Commands, as soon as I had settled what was necessary for my Departure.

At the Time of my dismissing *Dellius*, I had taken care to set off my Person to the best Advantage. No Art, no Ornament, no Grace was omitted, that might leave a strong Impression of my Accomplishments

plishments in the Mind of *Dellius*. I smiled, and looked, and spoke, as if I designed to gain his Affections though indeed all was intended; that he should represent and paint me in such amiable Colours to *Anthony*, as would make him impatient to behold the Original of so fair a Picture. Kings and Emperors, who could lay at my Feet Crowns and Sceptres, were the sole Objects of my elevated Spirit and boundless Ambition. It was *Anthony*, as Sharer of the Third Part, or rather of Half the World, against whom I played the Artillery of Love. Had all the personal or acquired Qualifications which were ever divided amongst Mankind, been centered in One, even that Man could not have inspired me with Love; nor should I have been any otherwise pleased with his Perfections, than as they enhanced the Glory of my Conquest.

As soon as *Dellius* was gone, my Imagination roved through the Variety of Pleasures the extensive Power of *Anthony* could invest me with. The many Kings and Princes, who, I was informed, attended in *Asia Anthony's* Levee, and waited his Nod, seemed now to my extravagant Fancy as Slaves to my Will, and Dependents on my capricious Humour.

CLEOPATRA.

I was however resolved to be slow in setting out on my Expedition, as first to be apprised whether *Dellius* had, according to my Expectations, raised in *Anthony* any eager Desire of seeing me. I therefore waited, till frequent and reiterated Messages were sent to demand my Appearance. At last the important Day came, on which my Fate depended. The Confidence indeed I had placed in my own Charms was so prevalent, that my Hopes of Success greatly outweighed and overbalanced my Fears.

I made what I thought the necessary Preparations of Money, Gifts, and valuable Ornaments; but in my own Person lay my chief Assurance. It was therefore this I was most sollicitous to adorn in such Manner as my Imagination flattered me would, with most likelihood, engage and conquer the Heart of *Anthony*.

I embarked on the River *Cydnus* in a small Galley; the Head of which shined with inlaid Gold. The Sails were of Purple Silk: The Oars were Silver, which beat Time to the Flutes and Hautboys. I lay under a Canopy of Cloth of Gold, curiously embroidered; and I was dressed as the Goddess *Venus* is usually represented. Beautiful young Boys, like Cupids,

Cupids, stood on each Side to fan me. My Maids were attired like Sea-nymphs and Graces; some steering the Rudder; some working at the Ropes. The Perfumes diffused their Fragrancy from the Vessel to the Shore. How did my Heart leap for Joy, when I beheld that Shore covered with Multitudes of People, who ran out of the City to view so uncommon a Sight! It seemed to me that I was received in Triumph; for *Anthony* was left alone, sitting in the Forum on his Tribunal; whilst all his Attendants flocked round *Cleopatra*, as their Queen. As I passed along, I heard a Rumour that *Venus* was come to feast with *Bacchus*, for the common Good and Security of *Asia*.

As soon as landed, *Anthony* sent me an Invitation to Supper. I considered some Moments what Answer to return; for I knew it was necessary to be very circumspect concerning the first Interview. I had Art enough to be sensible on what Trifles sometimes depends a Woman's gaining or losing a Conquest.

My Situation was such, that I dared not positively refuse *Anthony*'s Request; and yet I thought, that by keeping up the Dignity of the Queen, and by exacting

ing the Respect due to a Woman, I should be most likely to dazzle him with my first Appearance. I feared that by paying too hasty an Obedience to his first Summons, I should lessen the Awe which my Beauty might otherwise inspire; and which seemed equally proper to engage his Love, and to flatter my own Pride. As I wanted to make him think my Heart a greater Prize than any Kingdoms he could conquer, I took all possible Care to preserve my Dignity, and to raise at least a Shew of Difficulty in the Conquest. Instead, therefore, of attending him on his Summons, I sent him an Answer, That altho' as a *Roman* Senator, and as the greatest Man on Earth, he might demand Attendance from all the Potentates in the World; yet, as a Woman and a Stranger, I hoped the brave *Mark-Anthony* would so far indulge my Request, as to honour me first with his noble Presence.

The Emperor politely obliged me by his Compliance; and I had nothing to do but to prepare for his Reception; which I gave Orders for, with all the Elegance the Shortness of the Time would admit.

I contrived every thing as much as possible to weaken and enervate the Mind, and to make wanton Pleasures the most desirable. Soft Music was properly adapted to raise and sooth the Passions. A Number of Branches, with Lights in them, ingeniously disposed, some in Squares, and some in Circles, were let down at his first Entrance. Birds also were perched amongst the Branches, which, deceived by the Splendour of the Light, chirrupped and sung as if it had been Noon-day.

On each Side as he passed were placed beautiful Women, adorned to the best Advantage. The plainest of these stood first; and thence every Step he took, Beauties of a more exquisite Kind, and more richly dressed, attracted his Eyes. This I contrived to excite in his Mind an Idea of the Gradation of Beauty from the lowest to the highest Degree; and so certain was I of the Pre-eminence of my Charms, that the Charms of no other Woman were capable of giving me the least Jealousy or Suspicion; and I always took care to have the most celebrated Beauties about my Person; where they served as a constant Offering to my Pride, by shewing me, in my own Opinion, how much I excelled the fairest of my Sex.

CLEOPATRA.   23

I placed myself in a pensive Posture, with my Head reclining on my Hand, in such a Position that *Anthony* might see me, whilst he knew not that I could behold him. The first Moment it was apparent that I saw him, I rose with an Air of such Alertness, to meet and welcome my Guest, that my Foot slipped, as it were by Accident, and I fell on my Knees. *Anthony* flew to raise me; and as soon as it might be thought I could recover the Fright, which I affected to be in at my Fall, I thanked him, and said, I hoped this Accident, at our first Interview, was a good Omen, that by his Strength he would support a Woman's Weakness, and defend a Queen who resigned herself to his Power.

It is scarce to be credited how good an Effect this little Trick (trifling as it may appear) had on the Mind of *Anthony*. I read my Success in his Eyes, and inwardly applauded my own Wisdom. My Fall and Fright moved his Pity; whilst the Turn I gave it raised his Admiration, and at the same time reminded him of his own Greatness. He little imagined how this was in Reality an Omen, that by Tricks and Deceit I should rule him for the Remainder of his Life. The Emperor supported me by the Arm (for I still pretended I could not walk without Assistance)

Assistance) and led me to a Chair of State, which I had prepared for him. In this he placed me, seemingly against my Will; though indeed nothing could have pleased me more.

He sat by me; and I had had Experience enough in the Ways of Men, clearly to perceive that I had succeeded even beyond my warmest Hopes. *Anthony* was astonished and captivated with my Charms. His Voice faultered; his Words broke forth in trembling Accents; and he seemed at once to fear and to adore me.

The Raptures which possessed my Mind at seeing myself thus Mistress of the very Soul of *Anthony*, were inexpressible; and it would be a vain Task to pretend a Description of them. I omitted no one Art in my Power to increase his Flame; for as I had no Passion for him, my Judgment was cool, and enabled me to turn his Passions to my own Advantage as I pleased. *Cæsar*, it is true, had loved me as a Woman; but *Anthony* seemed to worship me as a Goddess; therefore I was better pleased with *Anthony*; though if I gave Preference to the Person of either, it was to that of *Cæsar*.

The

The next Night *Anthony* invited me to Supper; and I then fixed my Chains so strongly on him, as put it out of his Power ever to loosen them again. He informed me, that whilst he served in *Egypt* under *Gabinius*, my Youth and Beauty had exerted all their Force over his Heart; but as he was at that Time in a Station which made him despair of Success, and as he had no Means of declaring his Passion, he was obliged to stifle it; but that the Impression he then received was the Cause of his being now so earnestly desirous of beholding me.

It was true, that *Anthony*'s Station, when he was in *Egypt* with *Gabinius*, placed him much below my Notice; but yet I now thought proper to persuade him, that even the cursory View I then had of him, was sufficient to engage my Heart, and make our Desire of seeing each other reciprocal. The Improbability of this Story was no Bar to *Anthony*'s Belief of it: Nay, on the contrary, the more astonishing it was, with the more Eagerness did he seem to give it Credit.

As soon as I was convinced my Conquest was secure, with all the Wit and Pleasantry I was Mistress of, I demanded Rewards of *Anthony* for the

E   Assistance

Assistance I had sent *Dolabella*; not mentioning a Word that my Lieutenant in *Cyprus* had declared for *Cassius*: For when I was satisfied *Anthony* dwelt on the Words of the Speaker, without considering the Matter spoken, I dropped or added what Circumstances I pleased. An Artifice I made use of ever afterwards, in my Intercourse with the amorous Triumvir.

Anthony was very apt to place a full Confidence in the Integrity of others: A fine Disposition to be managed by a Woman he liked! He was naturally sincere, though somewhat slow of Apprehension; but as soon as he was made sensible of his Faults, much troubled, and ready to ask Pardon of those he had offended. This was true of him in general; how then would he fawn and cringe when he had offended his Mistress! It was impossible for a Woman of my Pride or Ambition to have met with a Lover more suited to indulge her Inclinations.

His Raillery was very sharp; but the Edge of it was taken off, and rendered inoffensive, by his suffering any Kind of Repartee; for he was as well contented to be handsomely rallied, as he was to rally others. This Disposition was the best calculated for
Treachery

Treachery to work on; for the Freedoms that were taken with him, on his own Permission, he imagined arose from open Honesty; and therefore could not fear Deceit from those who dealt thus freely with him. Besides, this Kind of Half-satire is one of the most refined Flatteries, when it is made use of to those whose Power over us is acknowleged; as it plainly conveys the highest Compliment to the Persons who condescend willingly to grant such Liberties to their Inferiors.

I observed that great Use was made of this Liberty in Business of Importance; for, upon examining any Difficulty, his Flatterers ordered their Affairs so as they might seem not to yield to him out of Complaisance, but because he had a Reach above, and a Penetration superior to, others.

Anthony was, as I have said, naturally of a very open Disposition; and this being improved by Love, could scarce fail of producing his Ruin, when his Love had once enslaved him to a Woman of Art; who considered him only as the Means of satisfying her Ambition, or indulging her capricious Humour, without having Affection enough for him to make his Interest, his Honour, or his Happiness, Points worthy her Consideration.

Such then was his Fate at present. For notwithstanding all the Appearance of Fondness which I put on, and which I acted to a degree of Perfection that must have imposed on any Man, who was in Reality what I affected to be; and notwithstanding all my warm Expressions, which carried Love up to Extravagance, and almost to Madness; I had, in plain Truth, no other Value for this great Hero, than as he was the Means of my Power, and the Instrument of my Ambition.

The first thing I did, as soon as I perceived my unlimited Sway over *Anthony*, was, as much as possible, to set him and all his Friends at Variance; for I knew his Friends must be my Enemies; as they, not being blinded by Love, as he was, would perceive my Intentions of continually deceiving him. Besides, I considered that I should have double the Trouble to persuade him to follow my Advice, whilst he conversed with others who would be perpetually persuading him to act the contrary Part. And as I did not care to trust him to the Conversation of those who were really his Friends, so I did not chuse
that

that he should have too frequent Opportunities of conversing with himself.

I placed therefore all my own Creatures about him; and thus, instead of fearing Opposition, I was always secure of having my Counsel well seconded, by those who were as indifferent as myself to any ill Consequences which might attend *Anthony* from following it.

For Example; *Anthony* was somewhat hasty in his Temper; and if ever that drove him to be unreasonable to another, I was sure to throw the Blame in the wrong Place, in order to justify and bring him into good Humour with himself; till he admired my Judgment, and was in Raptures at my Love for him. On the contrary, if any one dared to offend me, or even not to pay that Deference to my Dignity I thought it deserved (which, by the way, was almost impossible), I made *Anthony* abuse and treat them ill, only because it was my Pleasure it should be so: Nor did he even presume to ask what was the Nature of their Offence; because he knew that would put me out of Humour, and I should reproach him with not having Faith enough in my Understanding to
depend

depend on my Judgment of diftinguifhing Right from Wrong.

Thus he returned a little Flattery, which coft me nothing, by foothing my Humour, at the Expence of his Friendfhip, his Honour, his Juftice, and his Underftanding. But what fealed him moft firmly my Slave, was his greedy Love of Pleafure; for as my Smiles were his Satisfaction, and my Frowns his Torment, this placed him quite in my Power; fince I could inflict the latter, or indulge him in the former, juft according to my ambitious Will. And as I had fo little Love for him, that any Sufferings of his could not move me to Compaffion (nay, on the reverfe, when he fuffered on the account of my ill Humour, the Power of making him fuffer gave me Delight), I could command myfelf to plague or pleafe him, juft in Proportion as I thought neceffary to bring about my own Purpofe: For whilft he was in Agonies, I was unconcerned; and confidered only to what Advantage I could turn fuch his Agonies and tumultuous Paffions.

My Reflections on *Anthony*'s paft Conduct gave me Leave to hope, with great Reafon, for my Succefs with him in any Wickednefs I had an Inclination to perpetrate;

petrate; for whatever good Difpofition he might originally be endowed with, he had fo long accuftomed himfelf to follow the Bent of his Humour, without any Regard to the Juftice or Injuftice of his Actions, that he was the fitteft Inftrument I could have found to carry my pernicious Schemes into Practice. This his having a Hand in the cruel Profcription at *Rome*, after the Death of *Cæfar*, and efpecially the Murder of *Cicero* (a Man who had gained the general Efteem of his Countrymen), fufficiently proved; and I was refolved to make ufe of my Knowlege of his Character.

The firft Action of any Importance by which I exercifed my Authority, as I may properly call it, over *Anthony*, was the prevailing on him to put to Death my Sifter *Arfinoe*; which I effected, without even afking him to do it, in the Manner following.

Arfinoe was my younger Sifter; and to her, in Conjunction with my younger Brother (whom I poifoned, as has been already related) was formerly allotted the Kingdom of *Cyprus* by *Cæfar*.

The Character of *Arfinoe* was unexceptionable; and I never heard her mentioned without great Encomiums

comiums on her Goodnefs, as one Inftance of her Happinefs. This, befides that I wanted her Kingdom, ftung me to the Soul with Envy; and I could enjoy no Quiet whilft fhe was alive.

Anthony, for a Week together, found me frequently in Tears; and all he could get from me was fome Story I had invented of *Arfinoe*, as if fhe intended by Treachery to take away my Life, becaufe I was fo happy as to pleafe him. This I did fo often, that at laft *Anthony*, who would fooner have facrificed the whole World, than have feen me in continual Difcontent, fent in a Rage, and ordered *Arfinoe* to be deftroyed.

When *Anthony* told me what he had done, altho' I was in myfelf much pleafed, yet I fell into the moft violent Paflion imaginable; and, to prove my Goodnefs, faid, that though *Arfinoe* had plotted againft my Life, yet I could have forgiven her :---That I did not intend he fhould have known what vexed me; but he infifted on it; and I could deny him nothing: That I did not imagine he would have made fo barbarous an Ufe of my Confidence in him, as to deftroy my only Sifter. Then I ftamped, cried, and fhewed all the Marks of Agony I could poffibly devife;

CLEOPATRA. 33

devife; whilft *Anthony* fubmitted, begged Pardon, and tried every Method he could invent to appeafe my Anger. I carried this as far as it would bear, till I faw his Patience at an End; and he began, in his Turn, to ftorm, and rave, and rail, at Women. Then I knew he was provoked; for, whenever I difpleafed him, to avoid directly abufing me, which his Love would not permit him to do, his Rage vented itfelf on Women. However, I did not venture to urge him farther at this Time, but fmiled him into Peace. I made him believe my exceffive Grief for my Sifter prevented me from duly reflecting, that nothing but a Senfe of my Danger had infpired him to do what I had, perhaps, unjuftly condemned; fince, though my Sifter was dearer to me than my own Life, I was convinced my Life was, if poffible, dearer to him. Then, with a Sigh, and looking at him with an Air of great Tendernefs, I added, My *Anthony* fees how induftrious I am to find an Excufe for him; and if I could find none, he was fenfible I muft forgive; but as he knew the Excefs of my Love and Weaknefs, I hoped he would ufe his unlimited Power over my Heart with Gentlenefs and Mercy, and not triumph over his Conqueft.

F
At

At thefe Words, *Anthony* in a Moment forgot all that had paffed. He loved me the better for my Affection in lamenting my Sifter, and admitted (for what then would he not have admitted?) as a farther Proof of my Clemency, my prevailing with him to forgive *Magabezus*, the Prieft of *Diana*; againft whom he was enraged, for having treated *Arfinoe* with the Refpect due to a Queen, whilft he fanfied her my Enemy; though indeed the true Motive of this my Clemency was, that although I hated *Arfinoe*, yet I thought her near Alliance with me intitled her to royal Treatment. But, as a Reward for fuch Goodnefs, the Emperor gave me the Kingdom of *Cyprus*; and was fo delighted with my being reconciled to him, and condefcending to forgive him, for doing what I myfelf had urged him by Craft to perform, that he was ten times more my Slave than ever. Thus in every Quarrel I came off victorious, and gloried in the Thought of what a Dupe I made of this lordly Mafter of the Third Part of the Univerfe.

The next Inftance of my unbounded Influence over *Anthony*, was the carrying him back with me into *Alexandria*, in Oppofition to all the powerful Reafons that could be offered againft it; for it was

with

CLEOPATRA. 35

with great Difficulty that *Fulvia* his Wife maintained his Quarrel at *Rome* againſt *Cæſar*; and the *Parthian* Troops were aſſembled in *Meſopotamia*, under the Command of *Labienus*, and were ready to enter *Syria*; but in deſpite of all Motives that *Anthony* had to the contrary, I led him in Triumph into *Egypt*; and detained him there like a Captive, notwithſtanding the many ſtrong Remonſtrances of his Friends to rouſe himſelf in the Support of his own Dignity and Honour.

Although (as my Deſign was to be Miſtreſs of the Kingdoms or Empires which *Anthony* could conquer) it may at firſt Sight appear baffling thoſe Deſigns, to prevent his following his Intereſt; yet had I very concluſive Reaſons for keeping him with me at this Juncture of Time.

I had not been long enough acquainted with him to be aſſured I had fixed him ſo ſtrongly as Abſence could not cure him of his Love. I knew one of the chief Reaſons that made his Wife *Fulvia* ſo eager to proſecute the War, was the Hopes of forcing *Anthony* from my Power; and I dreaded more the Loſs of my Slave, than his Ruin. I cared not for his Intereſt,

F 2 but

but as I myself might be the better for it; and, consequently, I thought the Loss of a Battle might be recovered again; but if I parted with him, and should lose his Affections, I might suffer what would have been to me the greatest of all Miseries, the hearing of his Success and Happiness, whilst I could not share it. I therefore determined to keep him at *Alexandria*, let what would be the Consequence. To this End I invented all the Sports and Diversions I could think on, to employ his Time, and make him forget every thing but the present Pleasures.

I instituted a Kind of Order, to which I gave the Name of the *Inimitable Life*, and we of the Order were called the *Inimitable Livers*.

The first and grand Rule of this Order, was to contrive such Variety of Amusements and Delights, as might take up our whole Time, and prevent all Thought or Reflection from daring to intrude upon, or interrupt, our Pleasures.

This was directly aimed at *Anthony*; as I knew his thinking in a serious Manner must prove fatal to my Schemes. I therefore did all I could to enliven his

CLEOPATRA. 37

his Imagination, and to gratify his Senses, that he might have no Use of his Judgment; for as my Views were all selfish, without any Regard for him, both his Judgment and his Friends were my chiefest Enemies; and therefore I was resolved to be beforehand with, and exclude them from, him.

In those Hours when *Anthony* was most serious, or in those wherein he was most disposed to Mirth, I could accommodate myself to his Humour in such a Manner as I knew most suitable to maintain my absolute Power over him. I continually accompanied him; played at Dice, drank, hunted with him, and when he was exercising in Arms I was always by him; called him my *Hector*, *Alexander*, *Hercules*, and by all the Name of the Heroes or Gods of Antiquity. We dressed ourselves in the Fashion of the Gods and Goddesses, just according to our various Tastes: And sometimes, to make yet a greater Variety, we went rambling about at Midnight, disturbing and tormenting People under their Windows; I being habited like an ordinary Woman, and *Anthony* in the Disguise of a Servant. Sometimes he would come home from these Expeditions ill treated, and severely beaten. I had the Art of turning even this to my own Advantage; for whenever he he was in this Condition, I took the Opportunity of affirming with an Oath, that, was he really in the Station his prefent Habit fpoke him, I would prefer him in my Love to all the Emperors in the World. This Flattery *Anthony* received with the higheft Pleafure; for he never once reflected, that if I had not wanted to impofe on him, it would not continually have run in my Head to have made him fuch Sort of Speeches; for, confcious of my own Truth, I fhould then have thought he was alfo fatisfied of it.

Thus did I ufe to play my Hero all manner of Tricks, by way of Diverfion and Raillery. Sometimes indeed till he was half-angry; but then I contrived fuddenly to turn it into a Compliment to him; which diffipated his Anger, raifed his good Humour, and ferved to increafe his Fondnefs.

I remember we went out together to angle; when *Anthony*, being fo unfortunate as to catch nothing, imagined I fhould think him but a bad Sportfman; and the Impatience of his Temper threw him into a violent Paffion: However, he gave fecret Orders to the Fifhermen to dive under Water, and put Fifhes, that had been frefh taken, on his Hooks; after which he drew fo faft, that I, who was too much accuftomed

in

in impofing on others, to be eafily impofed on myfelf, perceived the Deceit. However, I pretended for the prefent to be wonderfully furprifed at his great Luck and Dexterity; but told my Friends, in fecret, what had happened, and invited them all the next Day to be Spectators of a like comical Adventure; and they attended accordingly.

As foon as all were got into the Fifhing Veffels, and *Anthony* had let down his Line, I commanded one of my Servants to be beforehand with *Anthony*'s; and my Servant, being the nimbler of the two, dived firft, and fixed upon his Hook a falted Fifh, one of thofe which were ufually taken in the *Pontick* Sea. The Moment *Anthony* imagined he had a Bite, he drew up his Line, and the whole Company could not forbear laughing at the Sight of the falted Fifh on the Hook. I faw that *Anthony* looked confufed and difappointed, and that his Eyes fparkled with Rage; but this did not at all terrify me; for when he was thus angry, I could in a Moment turn him into a a good Humour; and therefore, with a fmiling Countenance, and the fofteft Voice I could fpeak in, I immediately, addreffing myfelf to *Anthony*, faid, Permit us, brave Sir, the poor Inhabitants of *Charos* and *Canopus*, to enjoy the Reputation of being fkilful

in

in this Art. Cities Provinces, and Kingdoms, are your Game. Wonder not, great Sir, that poor little Fishes fly from your Hook, when all Mankind fly before your Sword.

This not only appeased *Anthony*'s Anger, but the sudden Turn from Confusion and Disappointment to being pleased and flattered, visibly appeared in the Alteration of his Looks. Thus did I contrive to heighten his Passion by every trifling Incident Chance threw in my Way. I smiled, and frowned, was pleased and displeased, so judiciously, and mixed his Pleasure and Pain so artfully, that I perpetually kept up in him a Passion of one Kind or other. I well knew that to suffer him ever to be calm was more dangerous for me than it was often to provoke him to Rage; and the Transition from the Passion of Rage to that of Love was so very pleasing to such a Disposition as *Anthony*'s, that if I had made it my Study continually to humour him, he would not have been half so sensible of the Obligation. I every Day thought of new Schemes to entertain him with varied and additional Elegance; but yet I generally took some Opportunity, amidst these Entertainments, and in the Height of his Jollity, to affect being out of Humour, and suddenly to dash all his Pleasures,
which

which I could eafily perform. Then would he rave, fret, and be fo miferable, that if I had had one Spark of Affection for him, I could not have borne it; but as Power was my Purfuit, nothing could gratify me more than fuch Inftances as proved that I could rule and turn *Mark Anthony*'s Mind with a Look, a Word, or any the leaft Sign of Refentment. Indeed the Agonies of Rage which I fometimes excited by fuch Means, gave me fo high and perfect a Triumph, that to hide the great Emotions of Joy in myfelf, on thefe Occafions, was perhaps the moft difficult Tafk I had to encounter; and even this flattered my Pride, and added to my Satisfaction.

I remember once, that in the midft of one of our Revels, when we were habited like a God and Goddefs, feated in Chairs of State, furrounded by all our Attendants, I fanfied I faw a Fellow of *Anthony*'s, whilft he was whifpering his Companion, put on a fcornful Sneer at the Anticks I played to divert his Mafter. Whether the Fellow meant what I imagined, I never knew; but the very Fancy that he dared to think otherwife than I would have him, was enough to draw on him my Anger, and provoke my Revenge.

I immediately, from smiling, sporting, and playing, became serious, grave, and reserved: I frowned, and looked discontented. *Anthony* presently observed the Alteration, and would know the Reason of it; when, after much Persuasion, I pointed to the Man, and said, That Fellow has mocked and insulted me; adding, I wondered how any of his Attendants should presume to do so: Not without some Intimation that it was his Fault to keep such insolent Attendants.

Anthony began to be enraged, but did not seem provoked enough for my Purpose. I therefore threw myself into a violent Passion at his Indifference to my being insulted; and said, I supposed if the Fellow had even dared to look amorously at me, he would have forgiven him. I knew such an Hint, without considering whether the Fellow was guilty or not, would work my deluded Lover to Madness. Nor was I in the least mistaken: For *Anthony*, at this Word, flew from his Seat, and catching the Fellow by the Hair, with his own Hand beat him so unmercifully that he almost killed him. I never troubled myself what the Fellow suffered, nor how much *Anthony*'s Rage provoked him. I had my Revenge, shewed my Power, and was therefore satisfied. However, I was obliged to sooth *Anthony*

with

with Smiles and Good-humour, till he had forgot this Incident; but I obſerved that an Officer of *Anthony*'s, who ſat by, looked in Agonies at ſeeing his Maſter worked by Paſſion to ſo unworthy a Demeanor; and who could not help calling to and intreating him to forbear. I ſaid nothing then, but marked this Officer in my Mind; and within a Week took care to find ſome Pretence to have him diſcharged from *Anthony*'s Service. For a Man ſo faithful and ſincere in his Affection towards *Anthony*, as to be really grieved when he ſaw him act an unbecoming Part, was not the Man I choſe to have about him. I knew I deſerved *Anthony*'s Friends ſhould abhor me, and therefore doubted not but they did ſo. However, I took care ſuch ſort of Friends ſhould not come near him.

Whenever I wanted to diſplace from about *Anthony* any Perſon, whom I but ſuſpected of valuing his Maſter's Intereſt more than my own Caprice, my Method was to frown on and inſult the Perſon, till I had made *Anthony* uneaſy: Then, when I had wrought him to that State of Mind which I thought would ſerve my Purpoſe, I pointed out to him ſome Inſtance of his Uneaſineſs, which I imputed to his Diſreſpect of me. This ſeldom failed of provoking *Anthony* to

Actions as prejudicial to his Honour, as to his true Interest; which, when he had executed, he always placed to the Account of the Person who had suffered; and very readily agreeing to the Hints I often gave him, that Men who could thus take Opportunities of provoking him were his worst Enemies, he was certain of discarding the unhappy Sufferer from his Service. On all such Occasions I never failed to exaggerate the Tenderness of his Affection to me; and would frequently blame myself for not bearing the highest Insult, which the Envy drawn on me by this Affection might create, rather than hazard his own Ease and Quiet; but then I took care to insinuate how much his Honour was concerned in protecting me; and by imputing my Resentment entirely to the Love I bore to him, I never failed to endear myself the more, at the same time that I was working him to all my Purposes.

I was very cautious of permitting the least Advantage to be taken against me, as I was very sensible nothing but blinding *Anthony* to his own Interest could keep him in my Power. But I was in no great Danger of losing him, whilst I could in one Moment look or unlook whatever the wisest Men could dictate to him. I had turned all his Senses
into

into Confufion, and had now gained an abfolute Conqueft over him. Thofe who laboured againft me did but weave *Penelope*'s Web, of which I could unravel more in an Inftant, than they could weave in a Day.

This triumphing over the Endeavours of the wifeft and beft of *Anthony*'s Acquaintance, was a chief Part of my Delight. I had one Art which I conftantly made ufe of when I intended to accomplifh any Purpofe; namely, to conclude whatever Advice I gave him, with an Affeveration of my Sincerity; adding it was that alone could make me fpeak, fince I was confcious his own Wifdom muft enable him to judge better than it was poffible for a weak Woman to do; and therefore hoped he would pardon my Liberty in fpeaking, which arofe entirely from my Zeal in any Caufe that concerned him. To govern a Man by continually putting him in mind that one is too weak to govern him, is an odd Effect of Man's Capricioufnefs; but fo it was in Fact with *Mark Anthony*. For if I had once appeared to think I could find out any Scheme of which he was not capable, it would have ftruck him with the Apprehenfion that he had not in all Things the Superiority; and he would not have complied with any thing I defired: Whereas by thus echoing my Weaknefs in

his

his Ears, his own Strength was pictured in his Fancy, and good Humour was the Result of viewing that pleasing Image.

Anthony easily believed that I sincerely loved him; and without nicely weighing the Consequence, indulged me in all I asked; and my Influence over him was as unbounded as could be possibly aimed at or desired by my unlimited Ambition, and Love of Power. Thus did I, Day after Day, by little Arts and deceitful Contrivances, manage the very Soul of *Anthony* in such a Manner, that reiterated Accounts of Defeats, and ill Success, were lost in that Sense of Pleasure I perpetually kept awake in him; and to his deluded Fancy, the World seemed to extend its Bounds no farther than *Alexandria*.

During this Year which *Anthony* spent with me, I so accustomed myself to Treachery and Deceit, that at last I could not live a Day without inventing some new Stratagem to impose on *Anthony*; and even sometimes, when I had no sort of Purpose to work out of it, but the mere Pleasure of the Deceit. To exult in the Thought, and gratify the glorious Ambition of knowing it was in my Power to deceive, was often the only End of my Artifice; and I could

not

not help thinking myself much greater than the greatest Hero; whose Conquests must be gained by the Help of others, and in whose Triumphs his Soldiers have a Right to claim a Share; whilst by myself alone were all my Conquests won; and by my own Policy was the Man, on whom the World had fixed its Eyes, steered and turned, just according to my Will and Pleasure.

At length arrived two Messengers; the one from *Rome*, to inform *Anthony*, that his Brother *Lucius Antonius*, and his Wife *Fulvia*, after many Quarrels between themselves, had at last joined to resist *Cæsar*; but, having lost all, were forced to abandon *Italy*; and that *Cæsar* had made himself Master of *Gaul*, and had got into his Hands the Legions which were there quartered.

The other Messenger brought the direful News, that the *Parthians*, under the Command of *Pacorus*, their King's Son, assisted by *Labienus* and *Barzapharnes*, had made themselves Masters of *Syria*, and marched as far as *Jerusalem*; which they had sacked, and had carried away *Hyrcanus* the High-priest, with *Phazael*, *Herod*'s Brother, Prisoners; whilst *Herod* himself

himself was fled for Safety to the Mountains of *Judæa*.

This was dreadful News; for in parting with *Anthony*, I feared that I risqued the Venture of losing him; and yet to detain him, if he must sacrifice all his Kingdoms for staying with me, was by no means answering my Purpose. The Sight of *Anthony* was not what I languished for; it was the Power he could confer on me, that made me so eager not to lose my Conquest. I could bear the Thoughts of his going against the *Parthians*; but his going to *Italy*, where he might meet *Fulvia*, raised in me such Apprehensions as were capable, like the Sight of the Gorgon's Head, of turning me into Stone. For I reasoned thus with myself: If *Anthony* should go to *Italy*, and have ill Success, he might then as well remain in *Egypt*; I shall be blamed for detaining him so long; and yet be suspected of wanting Power to detain him longer. He will then indeed naturally fly to me for Refuge; but the conquered *Anthony* will not be the same in the Eyes of *Cleopatra*, as the victorious Triumvir; whose Nod the gazing World attends. No, then it will be my Business to make my Court to *Cæsar*; and yet perhaps that might

might be rejected. For the amorous voluptuous *Anthony*, and the politic ambitious *Cæsar*, whose chief Object, like mine, seems to be Glory, are two very different Sorts of Conquests.

On the other hand, should *Anthony* succeed, and *Fulvia* share that Success with him, what then must be my Torments? Not even *Cicero* could describe my Agonies. *Apelles* could not have painted my convulsive Anguish: It would have baffled the Power of his utmost Art: Nor could *Roscius* himself, in the Height of all his Glory, when crowded Theatres panted for Breath in the Contest which should get foremost to behold him, have represented to the Life the various Passions that would have agitated my Soul, and destroyed my Peace; never to have been healed, nor restored again. Die then, *Anthony!* perish all the World, cried I! e'er this should be *Cleopatra*'s Fate. My Mind, thus tortured, left me but a few Hours of Rest or Ease; for I had a Part now to play much more difficult than any I had yet encountered since my Acquaintance with *Anthony*. I was very unwilling he should lose his Power in *Parthia*, *Judea*, and *Syria*; as I looked on all the Kingdoms he conquered to be my own; and as to parting with him, whatever I pretended, it gave me no Uneasiness. I was therefore well satisfied that he should go against the *Parthians*; but my Dread was, that if I once suffered him to depart, he might steer his Course towards *Italy*, and by that means meet with *Fulvia*.

I knew *Fulvia*'s Disposition was very like my own. That she was a Woman of violent Passions; but that Ambition was predominant in her Mind, and that her Arts to detain *Anthony* were almost equal to mine. I was therefore much more afraid of her, than I should have been of any other Woman.

I was sensible *Anthony* was born to be a Dupe to Women; and therefore the Woman I should have least feared, would have been one, whose Affection to him was so sincere, that she did not desire to make him a Dupe. In such a State, the natural Talents he had to be imposed on, would have been unemployed; and I question much if he would have been happy in it.

My whole Mind was bent to keep *Anthony* from going to *Italy*; and when he mentioned his Losses there, I made light of them, as not worth his Notice. But when he mentioned his Affairs in the East, I always

always agreed with him, that his Presence there was of absolute Necessity: Adding, that whatever Torment I should suffer by his Absence, yet so much did I value him above myself, that I would not have my Happiness or Misery be of any Consideration against his Interest or Honour.

When by these kind of Speeches I had worked my Hero into an Admiration of my Goodness, and had so deeply fixed his Thoughts on my Love for him, that I found he was filled with Rapture, I took an Opportunity of mortifying him, by throwing myself into the most passionate Fits of Crying, tearing my Hair, beating my Breast, and exclaiming, that though I would not detain him to his own Detriment, yet he must pardon a Woman's Weakness, which forcibly prevented my enduring his Absence without suffering those Agonies, raised by that dreadful Prospect. Thus I first took care to impress on his Mind the Picture of my Goodness, and then to work his Passion with the Opinion of my tender Fondness. He was several times prepared to set forth, when by these means I kept him from his Journey. Although it was my Design to let him go against the *Parthians*, for the Reasons already mentioned, yet I could not help indulging myself a little while

while with these Proofs of my Power; as they were my greatest Joy on Earth. And I often had some Struggles in my own Mind, whether the Glory of detaining him at *Alexandria*, whilst the World, in different Parts, demanded his Presence, would not more than repay any Losses *Anthony*, that is to say *Cleopatra*, might sustain. I held him, as it were, in Chains; and was averse to let him be ransomed, tho' the Kingdoms he might conquer and bestow on me should pay the Price of that Ransom. In short, I was apprehensive the World would imagine he roused himself, and broke those Chains by Force, as too weak to hold him longer; but then, on the other hand, I considered that the Pleasure of keeping him Prisoner would be all entirely lost, when his Power ceased, and Kings and Kingdoms were free from his Obedience.

This last Consideration prevailed on me to suffer *Mark Anthony* to depart. He collected together two hundred Ships, and a considerable Army, all designed against the *Parthians*. But the three Days before he set out, I tormented him to such a Degree, that he would often say, if he lost the World he would not leave me in such Affliction. When he mentioned this, I insisted on his Departure; (and indeed, seriously.

ously, for I intended he should go); and whatever my Words were, the Purpose I really had at Heart, was always accomplished.

I started from my Sleep in pretended Frights, crying out, I had dreamed my Lover was surrounded by his Enemies, and in Danger of his Life. At other times I dreamed that *Fulvia* had snatched him from me; and bore him in Triumph back to *Rome*.

Thus I made my sleeping as well as waking Hours subservient to my Artifices. Then would *Anthony* swear the World should never tempt him to go; and I took these Opportunities of insinuating, that *Fulvia* had raised all these Commotions in *Italy*, for no other Purpose than to drag him from me: At the same time begging he would, on no account, think of steering his Course that way, but persist in his Designs against the *Parthians*. Thus did I, by some means or other, do nothing but teaze and vex him. I cried, hung upon, and tortured him in every Manner I could invent; and, odd as it may appear, I was extremely sensible this Method of working *Anthony*'s Passions was the Way to make him eager to return. For whatever Plague the seeing me in these Agonies might be to him, yet as they appeared to arise from Grief at parting with him, I knew that would leave an Impression in his Breast not easily to be effaced.

At length *Anthony* departed; Tears came into his Eyes, and he could hardly bid me Farewell. Tears of Sorrow they were to him, but to me of Joy; to view the Hero weep at parting, gave me a Pleasure not to be expressed.

As soon as *Anthony* was gone, my Mind was perfectly calm. I dried up my Tears; for I had now no Part to act, nor Passion to affect; and therefore, with my Women and Attendants, only sought how to divert myself, and amuse my Time.

If *Anthony* could have peeped in, and seen me thus composed, the Moment after all my pretended Grief, what must he have thought? I wished it could have been so; for I was delighted with the Imagination, that, whatever his first Thoughts were, I could soon have made him believe afterwards, whatever I had an Inclination he should. An Instance of which I had just given, when I made him believe all my Endeavours to torment him arose

from

from Love. I had blinded his Eyes to such a Degree, that he could not discern that (if I had really been sincere in my Professions of Affection, and the Necessity of his Affairs had demanded our Parting) I should have yet concealed my Sufferings as much as possible, in order to have palliated his: I should have put on all the Chearfulness I could be Mistress of at such a Juncture, and have hid my Sorrows within my own Bosom, till I could vent them without adding to his: Or if indeed a Woman's Weakness had not permitted me to have gone thro' this Part, with a Resolution equal to my Desire, a Tear might now-and-then unguardedly have started from my Eyes; but my Sorrows would never have burst forth in Torrents, so as to have overwhelmed him with my Sufferings. The Marks of true Affection are so very visible (as I now know), that it seems almost incredible how easily I could impose on *Anthony*, to misconstrue my affected Behaviour as an Instance of Love, when, in reality, all I did might have assured him, if he had not been so blind, that I was a perfect Stranger to the Passion, or, at least, that I felt no such Passion for him.

Now my Hero was gone, my Diversion was continually to bring to my Remembrance, by Variety of Sports,

Sports, how I had entangled the Soul of *Anthony*. If Fishing was my Choice, all the Fish which floundered on my Hook, were to me as so many *Anthonies*. If I went a Birding, when the little Creatures were entangled in my Net, Ho, ho, cried I, you are caught as safely as *Anthony* himself! And the Pain of the Fish on the Hook, striving to get off, or of the Birds endeavouring to disentangle themselves from the Net, was just Matter of as much Consideration with me, as the Pain my Humours and Tricks used to give the deluded Triumvir. Nay, I viewed him with the greater Contempt; for I considered that neither these Birds, nor these Fishes, took me for their Friend; whilst I could make *Anthony* believe, when I had used all my Endeavours to torment him, that Love and Affection were the Causes of all my Cruelty. Then I remembered the Compliment I had paid *Anthony*, on our first Fishing together, that his Game were Cities, Provinces, and Kingdoms; and I immediately turned that Compliment on myself; for if his Game was so noble, what then was mine; who, with one baited Hook, or one Cast of the Net, could draw to my Lure *Mark Anthony*, and all those Kingdoms, which, with so many sleepless Nights, and repeated Dangers, he had conquered? But these Sports continued not long; for as I had

taken

taken care to place Spies about *Anthony*, who constantly informed me of all that paffed, I foon heard the News of what I fo much dreaded, namely, that *Anthony* was bound for *Italy*, and was now at *Athens*, with *Fulvia*. Not all the horrid Spectres the heated Imagination of the Mind of Man can form, could ever ftrike more Terror into the Soul, than did this News into mine. I revenged myfelf on the Meffenger; I was as one diftracted; and the Words, that *Anthony* was with *Fulvia*, refounded every Moment in my Ears, and filled my Mind with Anguifh and Defpair. I ruminated what Courfe to take, and ftill could find none to pleafe me. I once conceived a Thought of going myfelf to *Athens*; and of trying the Power of my Charms to entice him from *Fulvia*, and lead him in Triumph back to *Egypt*. But then the very Sufpicion of its being poffible for *Fulvia* to detain him againft my utmoft Efforts, frightened me from that Defign, and confined me as effectually to *Alexandria*, as if I had been kept clofe Prifoner in Chains.

My Spies alfo informed me, that *Anthony* and *Fulvia* fpent their Time in mutual Reproaches. *Anthony* upbraided her with the dire Effects of her Rafhnefs; which, during his Abfence, had madly lighted up the Firebrand of War, had engaged his Brother *Lucius* in an unsuccessful Business, and had given *Cæsar* an Opportunity to augment his Glory, and usurp an uncontrouled Dominion over all the Western Nations.

I was pleased to hear *Anthony* was thus peevish, and displeased with the War; as I flattered myself that it might arise from his Uneasiness at being obliged to leave *Egypt*. But still I feared *Fulvia*, who, as my Spies acquainted me, inveighed bitterly against *Anthony*'s blind Attachment to *Cleopatra*. These Spies were ordered by me to set down and transmit, as well as possibly they could, her very Words; and, among many other Invectives of that enraged Woman, who wanted neither Spirit nor Eloquence, I received the following. " Whence,
" (said she) but from *Egypt* are derived all your Mis-
" fortunes? You, and your *Egyptian*, have been the
" Cause of them all. What Part remained for me
" to act, incensed as I was at your Neglect and
" your Scorn, but to throw all *Italy* into Confusion;
" in hopes, by the Necessity of your Affairs, to
" force you to return? Yes, I own, *Anthony*, and
" I glory in it, that for Love of you I have set the
" Western World in a Blaze; but the Flame which
" rages

CLEOPATRA. 59

"rages there is trifling, in comparison with that
"which rages in, and devours, my anxious Heart.
"Into what Misfortunes have you precipitated your
"Brother, your Wife, and your Children? How
"many Months have I waited, an Exile and Vaga-
"bond in *Greece*, expecting that some God, favour-
"able to my Designs, would break the accursed
"Charm which detained you in *Egypt*? At last,
"I see you again; but shall I find in you that Hero
"whose Ambition made him carry his Pretensions
"as far as did the great *Julius Cæsar*; whose Death
"you so nobly revenged, at the Battle of *Philippi*?
"Can I flatter myself that *Anthony*, the Lover, the
"Slave, of an *Egyptian* Queen, can preserve for
"*Fulvia* the Tenderness of a Husband? You are
"now returned to me! invest yourself again then
"with your antient Virtue, which quitted you only
"when I was shamefully abandoned. It is not yet
"too late to repair your Shame, or my own. The
"adopted Son of *Julius Cæsar*, knowing how to
"take Advantage of your inglorious Ease, has, in
"despite of you, rendered himself Master of all
"*Gaul*; governs without a Rival at *Rome*; and
"disposes of *Italy*, as directed by his own despotic
"Will and Pleasure. Rouse yourself then, *Anthony:*
"Let us face this *Cæsar* in Arms. I am accustom-

" ed to the Din of War; and will second you in the
" Combat with as much Resolution as I would set the
" World on Fire, rather than yield you to a Rival."

Though there were some Passages in this Speech which raised my Indignation, yet I was well enough gratified with the Recognition of my Power; and not a little pleased that the Woman, whom of all the World I hated most, should live under the greatest Apprehension of the Transcendency of this Power. Here, perhaps, my Pride a little deceived me: For it is certain, that I likewise feared in my Turn.

I dreaded *Fulvia*'s Spirit; for the passionate Expressions she made use of, seemed to me the most likely Method of regaining *Anthony*. This also disconcerted and perplexed me much, for I knew not which Way to act. I could not write to *Anthony*, and persuade him that all *Fulvia*'s raging Passion was nothing more than her Pride's being disappointed, because she had lost her Influence over him, and that the World saw her Charms were not strong enough to hold him; for supposing she really had the Affection she pretended for him, she would sooner have patiently submitted to the Injury he did her,

her, in loving another, than have ventured his Ruin, by declaring War with *Cæsar*, in order either to remove, or revenge, that Injury.

This, tho' true, could not come from me to *Anthony* (as indeed very little Truth ever did); for this would have been too dangerous a Step; since it might possibly have opened his Eyes, and have removed that Delusion which I had been endeavouring, from our first Acquaintance, to inveigle him with; for as I had no Affection for him, if I had once let him see the Falshood of all those Marks of Love, whereon he built his Opinion of my Fondness, my Deceit must have been for the future ineffectual; and consequently my Power, which was supported alone by this Deceit, must have fallen to the Ground. Nothing can indeed be so impolitic, as to mention the Word Deceit or Treachery to those whom we intend to deceive or betray; for what more likely than that they may hereafter turn those very Suspicions on ourselves, with which we have armed them against others? It is indeed the Interest of all those who practise such Arts, as much as possible, to conceal and to deny them.

This Subject, therefore, I dared not to touch upon. At last it came into my Head to strike the boldest Stroke that I believe was ever thought on, to inveigle and allure a Man from his Wife; which was to turn *Fulvia*'s Claim to her Husband into Ridicule, and prove to him that I had the greatest Right to his Affections. The more uncommon and extraordinary this Project appeared, the more I was delighted with it.

Fulvia was somewhat advanced in Years; and her Person, which had never equalled mine, now suffered so much by the Comparison, that it was impossible but *Anthony* must, on the least Reflection, perceive the Difference to my Advantage. This Advantage, which my own Opinion at least gave me as much as was my Due, emboldened me to the Undertaking, and might have indeed assured me Success, in any Attempt on a Man who had always shewn his passionate Attachment to the Charms of Beauty; and who had often, in my Presence, declared its Value to be inestimable. And if his Appetites were thus guided in his Youth, I had no Reason to suspect, that, as he grew older, he would grow less nice, or less desirous of this grand Incitement to his Passion. I therefore, on mature Deliberation, and with particular

cular Care how to place my Words, in order to bring about my own Purpose, wrote him the following Letter.

"How short is the Space of Time, (and yet how long, if the Minutes were to be counted by my Sighs and Torments?) since *Cleopatra* was at a Loss for Words to express herself to *Anthony?* My Heart would once have dictated Expressions of Love and Fondness so fast, that my only Difficulty would have been to have stopped my Pen; but now I am restrained by Fear, lest the married *Anthony* should be chid by his Wife for corresponding with an unhappy Queen, who thought her Fame, and all she held most dear, too poor a Sacrifice for the Heart of *Anthony*. Yet why should I be afraid? For at once to despair and to fear, is a Pusillanimity beneath the greatest Coward. I have been neglected---I have been abandoned by *Anthony*.---*Fulvia* his Wife calls him, and he must break from my Arms to obey her Summons; though he leaves me breathless and dying through his Barbarity. Is this the much-boasted Descendant of the noble *Hercules*, who scorning all Confinement from his Pleasures, peopled all Nations of the World with his Posterity.

"Rather

"Rather might I think some whining Priest to have
"been *Anthony*'s Ancestor, who, not daring to exert
"his own Liberty, would preach all Mankind into
"the same Confinement. Perhaps, in the Compa-
"rison between me and *Fulvia*, she may have so
"much the Advantage, that *Anthony* cannot guard
"his Heart from yielding to such Superiority the
"Prize. *Fulvia*'s Age, I doubt not, at present
"may afford her Prudence, and her Person will
"secure her Constancy. Noble Advantages for
"*Anthony!* who certainly wants his Wife's Pru-
"dence to direct his Conduct, and must be obliged
"to the Defects of her Person for her Constancy to
"his Love. I confess Youth and Beauty have none
"of these Pretensions to your Heart. I say Youth
"and Beauty; for, vain as it may appear to boast
"of them, in the present Case they ought to
"have their Weight; and as to Form and Cere-
"mony, let them have Place where the Contention
"is trifling, for I despise them. I am pleading for
"the Heart of *my Anthony*, for I will not call you,
"or think you, the Husband of *Fulvia*---The Hus-
"band of *Fulvia* may perhaps talk or think of Wife
"and Prudence. He may, perhaps, be led to *Italy*,
"to maintain a War begun against his Consent,
"with a Design only to force him from his Pleasures.
But

" But this poor, this tame, this---Husband, is not my
" *Anthony*, is not that noble Triumvir whom *Cleo-*
" *patra* first met in *Cilicia*, and who could charm,
" even at Sight, a Queen in the Bloom of Youth,
" and the Height of Beauty. The Husband of *Fulvia*
" then is an Impostor; a Counterfeit; and I will
" seek my own *Anthony*, my Love, and my Empe-
" ror through the World, that I may again be blest
" with his Presence. But alas! it is in the Husband
" of *Fulvia* I must find my Love, my Hero, descend-
" ed from *Hercules*, and the Glory of his Race.---
" Find him, did I say?---No---it is in the Husband
" of *Fulvia* I must lose him for ever: For *Fulvia*
" will set the World on Fire, rather than yield him
" to her Rival. Nor is she the first neglected Wife,
" who, to destroy the Pleasures of their Husbands,
" would burn the World, and perish herself in the
" Flames. *Fulvia* would hold you by the Marriage-
" chains, because she has an Appearance of Right
" on her Side, and has not Charms to make ano-
" ther Conquest. But *Cleopatra* would hold you
" by your own Inclination, and would despise, for
" your sake, the whole World; at a Time when
" half that World would be glad to worship and
" adore her, to obtain the Favours she has shown
" to the ungrateful *Anthony*. Go, then: Prefer
" this

" this *Fulvia*, who defires to keep you fettered in
" the nuptial Chains. Prefer her, I fay, in the De-
" cline of her Years, and in the Decay of her Per-
" fon; prefer her to *Cleopatra*, in her Bloom of
" Youth and Beauty; when, tho' a Queen, fhe
" condefcends to court your Affections, and at the
" fame time acknowleges the Freedom of your
" own Inclination. But hold---what have I been
" faying? Oh *Anthony!* don't take me at my
" Word. I did not mean to leave you to your
" Choice, to prefer *Fulvia*; for that Moment which
" convinces me of fo fatal a Misfortune, will drive
" me to Defpair, and will fend me to the Grave,
" with all the Agonies that attend the Difappoint-
" ment of a Paffion which was once fo pleafing to
" *Anthony*, and still enflaves the Heart of

" CLEOPATRA."

I touched in this Letter on all the Points I thought moft likely to work *Anthony* to my Purpofe. I knew there was nothing he fo much delighted in as being reputed the Defcendant of *Hercules*. I therefore took care, in the ftrongeft Terms, to lay before him, that the only Means to make the World believe that *Hercules* was his Anceftor, was to follow
his

his Example; at the same time throwing in a Stroke of Scorn against the Man who would be confined from his Pleasures by the Laws of Decency or Sobriety.

The Force that lies in the artful Use of Epithets is almost incredible. The Word Whining, Canting, or any other which carries with it the Mark of Contempt, joined to the Name of Priest, has, perhaps, had more Effect on the Minds of Men, to give them a Contempt for the Doctrines taught by Priests, than would at first Sight be easily credited.

I had accustomed *Mark Anthony*, from the Time I had known him, to judge by the partial Glass of a heated Imagination, and to lay aside his Reason, as an impertinent Intruder on his Pleasures. I therefore could raise what Pictures I pleased in his Mind, and make him see them in that Light only which would best serve my Purpose. The Comparison I had drawn between my Person and that of *Fulvia*'s, I knew would engage *Anthony* in my Favour; which made me so often repeat the Words Youth and Beauty, to make the stronger Impression on his Fancy, in order to allure him to receive an Observation so new and uncommon, as that it was very unreasonable

reasonable in *Fulvia* to pretend to any Right in her Husband. The Ridicule cast on her Person was the only Method I could take to blind the Eyes of *Anthony*.

Oh! Ridicule, thou great Friend of us the Deceitful! who givest us more effectual Assistance to impose our Fallacies on our Dupes, than all the other Instruments of Deceit in the World. How did I worship thee in my Mind, whilst I was writing this Letter! in hopes to impose on the amorous Triumvir the most glaring Falsehoods that could be imagined. In short, my Business was to fix *Anthony*'s Thoughts on the Charms of my Person, till his greatest Inclination should be to do *Fulvia* an Injustice by abandoning her; and then to persuade him it was impossible for him to do her any Injustice, since Charms weak and decayed as hers were, could have no Right to claim the Heart of this Descendant from *Hercules*, this Emperor of the World.

Whilst my Messenger was gone with this Letter, I spent my Time in much Anxiety. For I concluded, that on the Success of this Scheme all my Hopes depended.

But

CLEOPATRA. 69

But I succeeded even beyond my Expectation; for nothing could have pleased me better than the Account my trusty Messenger delivered to me, unless he could have brought the Emperor himself with him to bear Testimony to the Power of my insnaring Lines.

The Messenger informed me, that *Anthony*, on hearing *Octavius Cæsar* had married *Scribonia*, the Sister of *Libo*, *Pomp y*'s Father-in-law, for the sake of his Shipping, advanced towards *Italy*, without shewing the least Concern for his Wife, whom he had left sick at *Scyon*, and whom he had not even deigned to visit before his Departure.

I asked ten thousand Questions in what Manner *Anthony* received my Letter; for I knew by every Trifle how much his Heart was moved; and found that he received it according to my Wish; that he laughed at some Parts of it, and cried out, " There " spoke the Wit and Spirit of my *Cleopatra!*" And when he came to the latter Part, wherein my Expressions were passionate, he kissed the Paper, and swore, that such Love and Tenderness deserved him All! That he would not for the whole World be so ungrateful as to let me suffer the Fate I seemed to dread.

dread. The very Idea of my Sufferings moved him so much, that he dropped a Tear; then bid my Messenger bear me back his kindest Love, with all Assurances of his Constancy; at the same time sending me a Jewel of an immense Value, as a Token of his Favour and Regard.

Henceforth I had no farther Fears from *Fulvia:* For now *Anthony*'s Inclination had prevailed on him to believe his Gratitude obliged him to prefer me to his Wife. I thought there was very little Reason to have any Apprehensions of her ever regaining him. This last Neglect of *Anthony*'s finished what his Infidelity had begun, and broke *Fulvia*'s Heart. For she was a Woman of remarkable Pride and Ambition; of a restless and turbulent Spirit; and could but ill brook such Treatment from a Husband, who had once been as great a Dupe and Slave to her, as he was now to me.

I could not abstain, in the midst of my Joy for *Fulvia*'s Death, from reflecting on the Possibility of such Treatment becoming one Day my own wretched Fate; but the great Faith in my Charms, assisted by my Art, soon drove all such Fears from my Bosom; and I looked on myself now as in the Possession

session of *Anthony*'s Heart without a Rival. I heard he had made a League with *Pompey*, and began to flatter myself he would conquer *Cæsar*, and be Master of the World; the Consequence of which, I doubted not, would be my being Mistress of it. Nay, I went so far as to lay Schemes how I should manage all the Kingdoms I should have in my Power. For as to the Word Give, I was as much a Stranger to it as the most tenacious Miser in the World. All my Care therefore was to manage in such a Manner as to keep all the Kingdoms *Anthony* gave me to myself, and let others share with me as little as possible.

I now abstained some short Time from sending to *Anthony*; for as I thought myself secure of him, I did not chuse to make myself too cheap in his Eyes. I would have *Anthony* believe me fond of him, and to esteem that Fondness to be the most valuable Thing he could obtain. To which Purpose it was necessary to preserve in his Mind an Idea of my Greatness, as well as of my Beauty. However, altho I did not send him any immediate Messages, yet I had Spies about him, who were to acquaint me with all Particulars of any Moment.

Ventidius

Ventidius had now conquered the *Parthians*, as *Anthony*'s Lieutenant, and freed *Syria* again from their Dominion. *Anthony* himself was besieging *Brundusium*, the Gates of which had been shut against him by *Cæsar*'s Order. Whilst *Sextus Pompeius* invested *Thurium* and *Consentia*, two Towns in *Brutium*. I thought all things looked well on *Anthony*'s, and consequently on my Side.

Cæsar's Troops, which had been in the Battle of *Philippi*, when *Anthony* was one of their Commanders, were very unwilling to fight against him, and said, they owed him too much to become his Enemy.

This Disposition of the Soldiers I hoped would either facilitate a Victory on *Anthony*'s Side, or promote such a Peace between him and *Cæsar*, as would not be to his Disadvantage, and give him Leisure (for I did not doubt his Inclination) to return to *Egypt*; where, when I could again inchain him, I was satisfied my Power over him was sufficient to make him lay at my Feet whatever Part of the Universe fell to his Share.

Whilst I was thus delighting myself with future Prospects, and basking in the Beams of imaginary Power,

CLEOPATRA. 73

Power, it was some little Time before I heard from my Spies at *Brundusium*. At last a Messenger arrived; but with such News, as was almost capable of turning me into Stone: For this Messenger informed me, that by the Means of *Julia*, *Anthony*'s Mother, and *L. Coccius Nerva*, a Peace was concluded between *Cæsar* and *Anthony*: That *Octavia* was made a Pledge of this Peace, by being married to the latter: That *Cæsar* and *Anthony* had entered *Rome* in Triumph, leading *Octavia* between them, in the midst of such Acclamations of the whole City and Army, as plainly demonstrated a more general Joy than had for a long time been known at *Rome*.

They had made a new Division of the Empire; by which it was ordained, that all the Western Provinces, taking in *Gaul*, should remain entire under the Dominion of *Cæsar*; and that *Mark Anthony* should be Emperor of all the East. *Codropolis*, a Town of *Illyria*, situated eastward of the *Adriatic* Gulph, on the Confines of *Macedon*, was to serve for a Boundary to the two Empires. *Lepidus* was to remain in Possession of *Africa*; and *Pompey* to continue his Dominion over *Sicily*, and some neighbouring Islands.

Thus,

Thus, in Appearance, the World was subjected to Four Masters; tho, to speak properly, the whole Universe obeyed *Cæsar* and *Anthony*; the Authority of *Pompey* over these Islands being very precarious, and that of *Lepidus* over *Africa*, as weak as the Spirit of *Lepidus* himself. So heartily did *Anthony* enter into this Peace, that he accepted the Priesthood of the new Sanctuary, erected to the Honour of *Julius Cæsar*, in order to please his Successor *Octavius*.

Amazement and Terror, at the Recital of this dreadful News, seized on my Senses, and almost deprived me of Life. *Anthony* was absent, and all Disguise was fled. Those Passions into which I used to throw myself, in order to work him to my Purpose (which were to appear to him as Vents to a Sorrow I did not feel), were now as unnecessary as they were impracticable. I was in so great a Consternation, that the Power of Speech was lost. If *Cicero* could not have described, *Apelles* could not have painted, nor *Roscius* have represented, the Agonies I should have felt at hearing of *Anthony*'s Success, whilst *Fulvia* was to share it: What then were my Torments, when I heard of his Success and Glory, when the young and beautiful *Octavia* was to share in that Glory? It might have been thought Duty was

Anthony's

Anthony's Motive to return to *Fulvia*; but *Octavia* appeared too much the Object of Inclination to admit that Thought. The raging Ocean only can give an Idea of my Mind, when I reflected, that *Anthony* lived, and was happy, and had escaped my Power: That he was married, and to *Octavia*: That he had entered *Rome* in Triumph with *Cæsar* and his new Wife, the Pledge of Peace between these Two great Men; who had saved the spilling much *Roman* Blood in a civil War, and was the Cause of Harmony and Concord between her new Husband and her Brother.

At length, when the first Consternation was past, disappointed Pride took its usual Course, and burst into Rage. I revenged myself on the Messenger who brought the News. With my own Hand I struck him; and would have stabbed him, if he had not escaped the Blow by Flight. I cursed the World, and vented my ill Humour on every thing around me: For though I looked on all those who came near my Person, so far dignified by the Honour, that they were above the Test of the World, yet I thought they were born to be Slaves to my Humour, and Objects of my capricious Power.

I often afterwards reflected on the Oddness of *Anthony*'s Fate. For this Dupe to the pretended Fondness of Women very narrowly missed breaking the Hearts of Two in the same Year, neither of whom had any real Affection for him. Such was my own Case; and as *Fulvia*'s Manner of Behaviour was so like my own, I made no doubt but that her Motives to such a Behaviour corresponded also exactly with mine.

However, my Pride afforded me One agreeable Thought in the midst of my Grief; namely, that I had no Love for the Man who dared thus to neglect me. I likewise found some little Comfort in the Account I heard of *Octavia*. That she was a Woman of the greatest Simplicity imaginable; who made it her chief Point to do her Duty, without being over-careful of the Consequence of her Actions; that if she had any Complaints, her Affection and Goodness rather inclined her to conceal them from those she loved, than to display them before their Eyes in their most dismal Colours, in order to be certain that she did not keep all her Sorrow to herself. That she had an excellent Understanding, but never exerted it in artful Tricks to impose on others; but was honest and sincere, wore no Disguise

guise herself, nor was apt to be suspicious of it in others; that she kept her Mind as free as possible from all Disturbance, and endeavoured to oblige, but never to vex, her Friends: In short, that her Mind possessed such Calmness, as arises from a Consciousness of doing Right to the utmost of one's Power.

It may appear very strange at first Sight, that this Character of a Rival should give me any Pleasure; but yet so it was, that such was the Disposition I desired in a Rival of *Anthony*'s Affections. For whatever Thoughts his own natural Judgment might have originally inspired him with, concerning the Marks of either Love or Goodness, yet by living first with *Fulvia*, and then with me, he had so long been used to the most gross Impositions, and had been so taught to mistake the true Symptoms of unaffected Passion, that I concluded it very probable he would be as blind to all *Octavia*'s Goodness, as he was to my Treachery and Deceit. Besides, before he could read clearly what Confidence *Octavia*'s Behaviour really deserved, he must have been at the Pains of ridding his Mind of all that Rubbish *Fulvia* and I had planted there. He must have confessed to himself he had been mistaken hitherto;

therto; and I imagined he would as soon undertake, like *Hercules* (his fancied Ancestor) to cleanse the *Augean* Stable, as attempt a Business so very irksome to his Nature; so that both his Pride and Indolence of Temper pleaded strongly for me. Another Hope I conceived was, that as on one hand I had accustomed myself to keep *Anthony*'s Passions continually disturbed, by fretting, teazing, and working him into Agonies, and then suddenly heightening his Pleasures, by changing the Scene from Ill-humour to Smiles and Complaisance; so, on the other hand, that *Octavia*'s submissive Endeavours to oblige would render him languid and insipid, for want of something to oppose the Bent of his Disposition.

A remarkable Instance of *Octavia*'s Simplicity, and her Faith in *Anthony* (although she knew of his former Correspondence with me), was, her giving herself no Trouble concerning my Spies, who continued to observe him, and informed me of all that passed. Every Person I had formerly recommended to *Anthony* was still pleasing to him; tho' I am not certain whether he had not forgot the Reason why he preferred them to the rest of his Attendants. For the Effect often remains in the human

CLEOPATRA. 79

human Mind, when the Cause is buried in Oblivion.

One Action of *Anthony*'s, whilst he stayed at *Rome*, gave me Hopes that I was not totally banished from his Thoughts; for on some frivolous Pretence he put *Marsius* to Death; but the true Reason was, he had exasperated *Fulvia*, by repeated Exclamations against *Anthony*'s Way of Life with me, and had stirred him up to War. This was so strong a Proof of the Event of the War, namely, his Marriage with *Octavia* not being so pleasing to *Anthony* as was generally believed, that I could not help rejoicing in it. For if there had been an utter Impossibility of my ever seeing or having any Power over him again, yet, if I could but flatter myself that he was unhappy, and made his Wife so too, by his Remembrance of me, it would have afforded me some Relief under the worst of Calamities.

Another Instance that *Anthony* loved those whom I had recommended, was, the great Faith and Confidence he placed in an *Egyptian* Astrologer whom I sent with him when he parted from me, as I imagined, for the *Parthian* War. This Astrologer, I believe, in Expectation of turning him towards *Egypt*, wanted to get him from *Rome*; and therefore declared to him that tho' the Fortune which attended him was bright and glorious, yet it was overshadowed by *Cæsar*'s; and advised him to keep himself far distant from that young Man. " Your Genius (said " he) dreads his. When absent from him, you are " great and brave; but in his Presence, unmanly " and dejected." And, indeed, so it did happen: For whenever they played at Drawing of Lots, or at Dice, *Anthony* was still the Loser; and as they often fought Game-cocks or Quails, *Cæsar* had always the Victory. This gave *Anthony* a sensible Displeasure. So that, quitting the Management of home Affairs to *Cæsar*, he left *Italy*.

But, alas! this Departure of *Anthony*'s did not answer my Astrologer's Design; for instead of turning towards *Egypt*, he took *Octavia* with him to *Athens*. However, I entertained great Hopes on finding *Anthony* was so jealous of *Cæsar*'s Superiority of Genius; for I doubted not but those Jealousies would, in Time, break into an open Rupture, and would make *Cæsar*'s Sister hateful to him: And that hence this Pledge of Peace would, against her Consent, and to her own Anguish of Mind, become the Firebrand to spread the Flames of a furious War.

It

It is incredible what Pleasures my Fancy formed from this Prospect. To imagine *Anthony* once again my own, to see my Revenge complete in what *Octavia* must feel, and to find all her Endeavours to preserve the Peace between her Brother and her Husband fruitless, must, to a Soul turned like mine, be more Joy than Words can express.

Anthony, whilst he was at *Athens*, led a Life so divided between Debauchery and Sobriety, that to those who knew but little of him, it was difficult to distinguish which was most predominant in his Mind; but I, who had been one of his chief Corruptors, and by my artful Designs of imposing on him, had made him so profligate, as to disable him from judging Right from Wrong, was very sensible his Debaucheries were his own, and that all Appearance from him of Sobriety or Decency, was owing to the Influence of his Wife *Octavia*. However, when I was informed that he often consorted with learned Men, or at any time gave himself Leisure to reflect, and that his Wife, by her Behaviour, gained the Esteem and Love of all the *Athenians*, it stung me to the very Soul.

But when I heard that *Anthony* had taken on him the Name of *Bacchus*, and would be adored under

M   the

the Denomination of *The God of Topers*; that he had a Temple near *Athens*, and erected a Throne in a Grotto which was called the *Cave of Bacchus*, where divers Instruments of soft Music were employed to enervate and weaken the Mind; my Hopes began to revive, and my Sorrow to be turned into Joy. To his Debauchery he also added the most insatiable Avarice; for the *Greeks* in Crouds prostrating themselves before the new *Bacchus*, supplicated him to take to his Wife *Pallas*, the Goddess and Protectress of the *Athenians*. *Anthony* complied with their Request, and consented to the Marriage, on Condition that the Goddess should bring with her, as a Dowry, a Thousand Talents. This Turn greatly surprised his Flatterers; and one of the *Athenians* told him, that *Jupiter* his Father exacted no Dowry of *Semele* his Mother. That is true, replied *Anthony*; but *Jupiter* was rich, and I want Money.

The same Feast was kept in all the Towns of *Peloponnesus*, and each contributed, according to his Power, to the Expences of the Marriage of *Pallas* and *Bacchus*. *Anthony* was so delighted with his new Dignity (which he took care should not be an empty Title), that he ordered the Name of *Bacchus*

to

to be inscribed at the Foot of all the Statues erected to his Honour.

Every Instance of Caprice, Avarice, and Debauchery, which I heard of *Anthony*, gave me infinite Satisfaction; both because I knew them to be the Fruit of my own Plantation in his Mind, and that *Octavia*, tho' the best and most indulgent Wife in the World, yet, as she loved him sincerely, and could not be pleased with what must end in his Dishonour, would find it impossible continually to keep him from the Woman, who not only complied with his Debaucheries, but daily invented new Ways to heighten the Gratification of them.

Anthony from *Athens* set Sail to *Syria*, where he settled some Affairs that stood in need of Regulation, and then he returned again to *Athens*. Here, being provoked with *Cæsar*, by some Reports he had received against him, he made no Stay; but sailed immediately for *Italy*, with a Fleet consisting of an Hundred Ships; and being refused Harbour at *Brundusium*, he made for *Tarentum*. There his Wife *Octavia*, who came from *Greece* along with him, and was then with Child, prevailed with him to send her to her Brother. She met *Octavius* by the Way, and had a Conference with him, in the

Presence of his Two Friends *Misenius* and *Agrippa*. By her Tears and Prayers, and intreating her Brother to consider her Misery, if War should ensue between him and her Husband, she so softened *Cæsar*, that he marched peaceably to *Tarentum*, where, with a powerful Army drawn up on Shore, and with a great Fleet in the Harbour, no one Act of Hostility was committed on either Part; nothing but kind Salutations and other Expressions of Friendship passing between one Side and the other. In short, *Octavia* again was the Cause of Peace between *Cæsar* and *Anthony*.

But whilst I was raving at the Disappointment of all my Hopes, every thing turned out much more agreeably to my Wish than the warmest Imagination could have flattered me with, or my highest Confidence of my own Charms could have expected; for it was at length agreed that *Cæsar* should give *Anthony* Two of his Legions to serve him in the *Parthian* War, and that *Anthony* should in Return leave with him an Hundred armed Gallies. *Octavia* moreover obtained of her Husband Twenty Brigantines for her Brother, and of her Brother a Thousand Foot for her Husband. So having parted very good Friends, *Cæsar* went immediately to make War with

Sextus Pompeius for the Recovery of *Sicily*; and *Anthony*, leaving with him his Wife and Children, together with the Children by his former Wife *Fulvia*, set Sail for *Asia*.

This Separation of *Anthony*'s from *Octavia*, seemed to me the only Means by which I could regain him. I had long ago wrote a Letter, which I trusted to one of my faithful Spies to give *Anthony*, whenever he should be absent from his Wife, who from the Time of that fatal Marriage, which caused me such incredible Torment, had, in Appearance, had so much Influence over him, that my Pride would not suffer me to venture the dreadful Fate of having my Passion, or, to speak more properly, my pretended Love, exposed under my Hand to a Rival, to whom, I knew, if *Anthony* was really fond, he would not scruple the making me a Sacrifice. For all Women who will not be contented, unless the Passions of their Lovers arise to Madness, and spur them on to be unreasonable and injurious to the rest of Mankind, must pay the Tax of being for ever uncertain how soon a Transfer of those Passions (which have no other Foundation than Whim and Caprice) may sacrifice them to the newer and more pleasing Object.

However,

However, as soon as *Anthony* was one Day's Journey from his Wife, my Spy delivered him my Letter which contained these Words:

"Language is too narrow, and Words are too
"weak, to express or convey to *Anthony* an Idea of
"what Havock and Desolation his Behaviour has
"made in *Cleopatra*'s tormented Bosom. Perhaps I
"am even now too bold and presumptuous in daring
"to address you under the well-known, the well-
"beloved Name of *Anthony*; and should make my
"Application with such Distance and Ceremony as
"is due to one of the lordly Masters of the Universe,
"and the Husband of *Cæsar*'s Sister. But forgive me,
"my *Anthony* (for so I must call you), as that Name
"brings to my Remembrance those happy Days,
"when Time itself flew too fast for our Pleasures!
"when in each other all our Desires were satisfied,
"and every Joy complete! Yet why should I wish
"to bring to my Remembrance what only serves to
"heighten the Sense of my present Misery? I know
"not; unless it be, that Passions, as strong as that
"which has long been fixed within my Breast, when
"disappointed, neglected, and despised, render us
"incapable of every other Comfort but of venting
"our Sorrows. Could Tears write as legibly as
"Ink,

"Ink, my streaming Eyes would, with an inex-
"hauftible Fund, affift me to fend you all my
"Woes, and pour forth all my Griefs. But think
"not I mean to move you to Compaffion; no---
"that were too much for the wretched Queen of
"*Egypt* to expect. And yet, methinks, fhould
"you deign to anfwer and comfort me but with
"One Line under your Hand, the Crime could not
"be very great. Or, if an Opportunity prefents it-
"felf, fhould you, in Pity, fuffer me once more to
"fee you (for I would fly to obey your Commands),
"I cannot think fuch Pity would be unbecoming
"the noble *Anthony*. But perhaps fuch a Con-
"defcenfion would be taken ill by the mighty *Cæfar*.
"He would fancy his Sifter neglected, and himfelf
"affronted. I confefs this Objection to my Requeft
"ftartles me; for I am told your Genius is daunted
"and affrighted when in the Prefence of *Cæfar*'s.
"Be therefore cautious that he grows not angry;
"and let not the unhappy *Cleopatra* be the Caufe
"of your offending the great and mighty *Cæfar*,
"who has found the Means to awe Mankind. I
"once thought *Anthony* could have been awed by
"no Frowns but thofe of his *Cleopatra*; but thofe
"Days are paft. To gratify *Cæfar*, and compofe
"his Frowns, *Anthony* muft be entirely devoted to
" *Octavia,*

" *Octavia*, and I must be the lost, the wretched,
" abandoned, neglected, despised, and, O! let me
" add what is sincerely true, the distracted

" Cleopatra."

Anthony in his Disposition had a great deal both of Pride and Compassion; but when the former intervenes, the latter must for the present subside; unless they have different Objects to work upon; for no Man can at once feel his Pride piqued, and his Compassion moved, by the same Object. I depended therefore more on those Parts of my Letter which tended to alarm the former, than on those which seemed designed to raise the latter.

This was indeed my last Resource. For *Octavia* was too young, too handsome, and too faultless in her Behaviour, for me to find any other Means of engaging *Anthony* to abandon her, and justify to himself his so doing, than by making him imagine she wanted to hold him by *Cæsar*'s Power. I did not fear but that if I could once move his Passions in my Favour, his Imagination would help him either to bias or to silence his Judgment; and I succeeded beyond

yond my Expectation. For when he read my Letter, at thofe Parts I endeavoured to excite him to Pity, he faid, " Poor *Cleopatra!* what muft you " have fuffered!"----But when he came to that Part which concerned *Cæfar*, he ftamped, bit his Lips with Rage, and cried out, " Shall *Octavia* " have me all, for Fear of *Cæfar*'s Frowns? No! " I'll fhew the World this mighty *Cæfar*'s Nod " may be obeyed by Slaves; but that *Anthony* " will fhare, not dread, his Power." Then he threw down the Letter, raved and railed at me, for imagining he was capable of Fear; and, for a Moment, feemed to harbour in his Bofom, even againft *Cleopatra*, a moft implacable Hatred. But when he had vented his Paffion in all the Fury Words could exprefs, his Mind took a fudden Turn. My Image prefented itfelf to his Fancy: He fnatched up the Letter again, and on perufing the Conclufion, in which I had fo ftrongly painted my Diftraction, he faid, " Oh *Egypt!* I will reward thy Con- " ftancy, thy Love, and Tendernefs; and let *Octa-* " *via* fee, that I am not to be awed, nor threatened, " into Love."

When *Anthony* had once got this Notion ftrongly in his Mind, that his Wife wanted to keep him by
the

the Terror of her Brother's Rage, he began to hate her, without serioufly confidering whether she was guilty or innocent, of what she was accufed by my Art, affifted by his own heated Imagination.

When my Spy, to whom I had intrufted my Letter, sent me Word in what Manner *Anthony* had received it, I wrote to him Day after Day, till he came into *Syria*; where, contrary to the Advice of all his Friends, and notwithftanding their Remonftrances, he fent *Fonteius Capito* to conduct me to him.

None but thofe ambitious Minds, which, after a long Defpair of Succefs, have at length arrived at the full Enjoyment of their mad Defires, can have an adequate Idea of my Tranfport at the Sight of *Anthony*'s Meffenger.

The whole Succefs of my Scheme, in piquing *Anthony* with the Thoughts of his Fear of *Cæsar*, gave me almoft as much Pleafure as did the Confequence of it in regaining his Inclinations. For as this was my own Contrivance, I applauded myfelf for the Ingenuity of my Invention. Which Self-approbation

tion is, perhaps, one of the highest Gratifications a proud and imperious Soul can indulge.

I flew to obey *Anthony*'s Commands; and, as soon as it was possible to make the needful Preparations, I set out with his Messenger.

My Thoughts were employed, during my Journey, in what Manner I should behave on my Arrival. I asked *Fonteius Capito* a thousand Questions about *Anthony*'s present Disposition; how he behaved towards *Octavia*; and what was now his Way of talking concerning Women in general? For I was well apprised that much was hence to be learned as to the Manner in which it would be most proper to treat him.

By *Capito*'s Answers, and my Knowlege of *Anthony*, I collected that his general Discourse concerning Women implied a Contempt of them; as if they were properly Slaves to Men, and could not be too submissive. As to *Octavia*, that notwithstanding her utmost Care and Diligence to obey even his minutest Commands, yet from the Carelessness of his own Disposition, and from the Simplicity of hers, he never believed she submitted to him at all.

I had

I had placed Spies enough about *Octavia*, from the Time of her last Marriage, to be perfectly acquainted with her real Character; and as I knew every Turn, and could trace the most intricate Labyrinths, of *Anthony*'s Mind, I could easily perceive that *Octavia* was so assiduous in her Endeavours to oblige her Husband, and was so chearful in her Compliance with him, that his Commands appeared to him to be her own natural Inclinations. In short, it was *Octavia*'s Study to obey him in Fact; and as she had no sinister Views in what she did, she never thought of making it a Point to place her Obedience so fully in his Sight, as that it must be uppermost in his Mind.

Octavia succeeded in her Design; for she obeyed *Anthony*. And now I resolved to gain my Project, by engaging him to believe that I obeyed him; whilst in Reality I thought of nothing but the Indulgence of my Inclinations, and the gratifying my Ambition. I understood the Art of making the utmost of all the Advantages Nature had given me. I could muster all my Charms, both of Person and Understanding. I could dress them in the most becoming Manner, and make them pass, as it were, in Review before a Man's Eyes, whenever I pleased.

As

As to Goodness, I could at any Time affect just as much of it as served my present Purpose, and was conducive to the accomplishing any of my favourite Schemes; and as this was Affectation, like a loose Robe I could turn and wind it, so as to place it in that Light which I thought best fitted to dazzle and blind the Eyes of the Man whom I intended the Honour of being my Dupe.

I was also much pleased by *Capito*'s Account, that *Anthony* did not see *Octavia*'s Actions in the fairest View. For when I joined this with the Reflection on his kindling so soon with my hinting his Fear of *Cæsar*, I began to hope that his Wife had never had any great Share in his Inclinations; but that the Desire of keeping Peace with *Cæsar* had indeed been the true Motive of his hitherto living well with her. I knew how to manage this Thought to my own Advantage, and resolved to have it ready to echo in *Anthony*'s Ears, whenever I could make it any-ways subservient to my own Interest. Thus, by forming in my Mind various Schemes how I should improve this my new Conquest (as I esteemed it) over *Anthony*, did I employ my Thoughts till we met.

Anthony waited not to receive me at home; but came to conduct me Part of the Way himself. The Joy that appeared in his Countenance at my Approach, is not to be expressed. I threw myself at his Feet in the most humble Posture, and put on so submissive an Air, as added to the Delight of seeing me again, after so long an Absence; and raised in his Mind the pleasing Reflection, that I was wholly in his Power, and had no Brother to fly to for Refuge, in case he should abandon me. This gratified him in all respects; for besides his apparent Inclination for me, it fixed him in the Opinion that he was engaged on my Side by every Tie of Compassion and Goodness. He made me a great many valuable Presents, and seemed to be as much my own as ever. But I forbore some time trying any great Experiments of my Power, lest by a too hasty Use of it I should diminish and destroy it. For the present, therefore, I only echoed my Obedience in his Ears, and was so very submissive, that I took care to make all my Words and Actions appear the Result of his Commands. However, in order to gratify myself with the natural Bent of my Humour, I was doubly insolent to every one around me. This Behaviour kept up in *Anthony* some Notions of my Greatness; and at the same time charmed him with the Idea

that

that all that Greatnefs was dependant on him, and in compliance to his uncontrouled Will and Pleafure.

I carried this on till I had fixed in *Anthony*'s Mind the Opinion of my obedient and fubmiffive Temper fo very ftrongly, that I thought it would be difficult for even a contrary Behaviour to root it from his Imagination. By degrees I began to exert again all my former Humours in the fame Manner as when he was firft with me at *Alexandria*; but yet he did not in the leaft difcover it, or perceive the Alteration. As an old Man, when his Memory begins to decay, retains ftill thofe Impreffions which in the Vigour of Youth were imprinted on his Mind, and yet forgets what paffed but Yefterday, fo *Anthony* greedily receiving the Impreffion of my Obedience, and his Fancy picturing it continually before his Eyes, whatever paffed afterwards had no Power to eradicate it. At the very time when every one elfe faw that I ftudied nothing but my own Will and Pleafure, he would infift and affirm, that his Pleafure was the principal, nay, only Object of my Study. When I found I had him thus fecure, I began to put in Execution the Defigns I had before intended.

The firſt Step I took, was to get rid of all thoſe Friends of *Anthony*'s who had adviſed him againſt ſending for me into *Syria*; and likewiſe of all thoſe who, as my Spies informed me, had favoured *Octavia*. And here I played my old Trick over again; that is to ſay, I uſed them with ſuch repeated Inſults, ſuch Arrogance and Ill-nature, as rendered it impoſſible for them to conceal their Anger; and the very Inſtant they preſumed to ſhew, by their Looks, that they were not even rejoiced at being abuſed, I made *Anthony* believe their Diſpleaſure aroſe from Diſreſpect to him, which cauſed their Hatred to me.

When by theſe means I had cleared *Anthony* of all thoſe Perſons to whom I had any Diſlike, and had ſatisfied my Revenge, my next Step was to endeavour to obtain ſome Gratification for that raging Avarice which poſſeſſed me. This I contrived to accompliſh by raiſing falſe Accuſations againſt the *Syrian* Noblemen and Governors. The Moment I took it into my Head to fancy the Poſſeſſions of others would be convenient to me, I invented ſome monſtrous Story of their Perfidiouſneſs and Treachery, of the Truth of which I was careful to convince *Anthony* by Ten thouſand Arts and Plots;

whilſt

whilft he ftood in Admiration of my Watchfulnefs for his Safety, and applauded my great Penetration in diving into all political Secrets. A Penetration indeed no Perfon could have attained with the utmoft Affiduity, joined to the moft univerfal Knowlege; unlefs, like me, their Invention fupplied the Want of Fact, and they could paint others in any Colours which beft fuited their own Defigns.

Anthony, by my Contrivance, ordered the Affaffination of *Lyfanias*, whom he himfelf had made King of *Chalcis*. My Pretence was, his taking Part with his Enemies; but my real Aim was, to be enriched with his Spoils. In fhort, *Cyrene*, *Cyprus*, *Cœlo-Syria*, *Iturea*, and *Phenicia*, with great Part of *Cilicia* and *Crete*, were all added to my hereditary Dominions, which (now I had again got Poffeffion of *Anthony*) I looked upon as a mere Trifle, in comparifon of that unbounded Power, and immenfe Treafure, my Fancy had beftowed on me.

But the principal Objects of my prefent Ambition were *Herod*'s Kingdom of *Judea*, and *Malchus*'s of *Arabia*: The former of whom I accufed of having governed tyrannically, and the latter of having favoured the *Parthians*. I had alfo another Motive,

O befides

besides the avaricious Desire of his Kingdom, which prompted me to endeavour to dethrone *Herod*, namely, his Fondness of his Wife *Mariamne*: For although *Judea* was granted to *Herod* by the *Romans*, yet by his own Bravery and Conduct he acquired the Possession of it.

Herod was a King celebrated for his Valour, and esteemed in the World as a great Man; and consequently I could not bear the Thought of another Woman's having any Power over him; for I looked on all the Kings, at least all the famous Kings, of the Earth, as born to be Slaves to my superior Charms. Nor did it lessen in the least my Enmity to *Mariamne*, when I considered I had great Reason to believe that she had no Fondness for *Herod*. For I looked on Deceit as so trifling an Expence, that the World's even imagining a Woman had any Influence over a Man who had a Kingdom at his Command, was, in my Opinion, more than a sufficient Reward for such Deceit.

It is true, *Herod* had begun his Reign with a barbarous and savage Action; for after having delivered the old *Hyrcanus* from Confinement, and granted him all royal Honours, he underhand

contrived

contrive that he should suffer a cruel Death. But this, though the pretended, was not the real Cause of my accusing him to *Anthony*. So far was I from considering Cruelty in its true Light, when it was perpetrated in order to obtain a Crown, that I should have despised the Man, as void of Spirit, who had hesitated a Moment the Overleaping any Bounds which barred his Passage to the ascending a Throne. However, this Affair was deferred for a little time; because the Season of the Year called *Anthony* to quit *Antioch*, and to march towards *Armenia*. I was very unwilling to part with him, fearing, by a second Absence, to lose my Power again; and notwithstanding all the Opposition that Reason could make to it, I would accompany him as far as the Banks of the *Euphrates*, where I made it so much his Employment to prevent my plaguing him with my Whims and Caprice, that he neglected, by these means, all the necessary Preparations for the War, which a much less experienced General (who had not been thus infatuated to the Charms of a Woman) could not have omitted. The nearer we approached to *Armenia*, the more strongly I renewed my Solicitations of obtaining the Kingdoms of *Judea* and *Arabia*.

Anthony was leading his Troops againſt a formidable People; and if he ſhould fall in that War, I was willing to be in Poſſeſſion of all that his preſent Power could inveſt me with. At *Laodicea*, *Herod* and *Malchus* attended the Triumvir, in order to juſtify themſelves from the Crimes laid to their Charge.

But with all the Arts I was Miſtreſs of, and all *Anthony*'s Partiality in my Favour, I could only prevail with him to take from *Herod*, *Jericho*, and the *Balſam Gardens*; and from *Malchus*, *Arabia*, *Nabath*, which is ſo fruitful in Perfumes. Nay, when I preſſed him farther, he at laſt grew ſo peeviſh, that he bid me mind my own Buſineſs, and not trouble myſelf any more about *Herod*.

This was the greateſt Rebuff I ever met with from *Anthony*, and the only Point in which I ever failed of Succeſs. The Diſappointment was very hardly borne by one of my impetuous Temper; nor did I ever forget it; but took every Occaſion to teaze and torment *Anthony*, the Remainder of my Life.

But although *Anthony* could not gratify my boundleſs Ambition, nor my inſatiable Avarice;

for

for if he had given me the World, with an Exception only of the minutest Trifle, I should have been dissatisfied; yet was he much reproached with his Profuseness towards me. He would often say, that the Greatness of the *Roman* Empire consisted more in giving, that in conquering, Kingdoms.

All the Reproaches that were cast on *Anthony* for my sake, appeared to my Fancy so many Trophies erected to my Honour; as they were Proofs of my Power over him; and, according to the Notions I had long fixed in my Mind, his Honour and my own were so incompatible, that I always thought as the one lessened, the other increased.

At length I was obliged to leave *Anthony*, whilst he pursued the *Parthian* War: But before I parted from him, I renewed all my old Tricks over again, and played the same Part as when we were separated before. One Moment flattering him with all the Marks of passionate Sorrow, in my being so unfortunately obliged to live a Day without his Presence; and the other, putting on the Height of Good-humour and Rapture on his being yet with me. I would sigh, and break forth in Exclamations on the curfed *Parthian* War, as the Caufe of my having once loft *Anthony:* Adding, that I fhould not then have parted with him, had I known he would have fteered his Courfe towards *Italy.* But fhould *Cæsar*, the mighty *Cæsar*, fend for him to *Rome,* and *Octavia,* by her Brother's Power, have again the Poffeffion of him, I could never furvive it.

When I faw *Anthony* was thoroughly grieved at parting with me, and that by giving him an Idea of *Cæsar's* fending for him (as being one of fuperior Power) he was deeply affected; then would I make a fudden Tranfition in his Mind, by fmiling him into Joy; and faying, there was no Caufe yet to grieve, for my *Mark Anthony* was yet with his *Cleopatra*; and I would referve my Grief, to vent it when alone.

Thus did I alternately work *Anthony* into Agonies, and raife him into Raptures, till I knew I had fixed my Image fo ftrongly on his Mind, that he would haften back with the utmoft Speed. We parted; but I did not keep my Word in venting my Grief alone. Indeed how was it poffible I fhould; for in Reality I had none to exprefs? And the Affectation

fectation of it vanished, as soon as my Hero was absent. Instead of grieving, it was my Study how to amuse and divert myself.

Judea ran much in my Head, because I was disappointed in the Possession of it, which, I believe, made me think of going thither. I visited all the principal Towns in *Syria*, and came at last to *Judea*. *Herod* treated me with the highest Respect, and seemed inclined to engage me in his Party, in case *Alexandra*, his Wife's Mother, a Woman of an ambitious turbulent Spirit, should give him any Disturbance by Complaints to *Anthony*. But I had Designs of my own; and was resolved to try every Method to obtain his Kingdom.

The first Thought that struck me, was to endeavour to inspire *Herod* with Love; for which I had Two Reasons. The one was, to free him from *Mariamne*, and have another King my Slave; the other, that I was sure this would be a certain Method of destroying him with *Anthony*; about whose Person I had placed my Friends and Spies in such a Manner, as I doubted not his being made believe that I was innocent; and *Herod*, tho' guilty, unsuccessful.

I had

I had accustomed the Triumvir to so much Fallacy, and had used him so long to think any thing true which he had a mind should be so, that I might very well depend on his Fondness for my own Acquittal. But I knew *Herod*'s Head must pay the Forfeit of *Anthony*'s once imagining he presumed but to think of me. Nay, I went so far as to believe it would make *Anthony* yet more my Slave, after he should have the dreadful Idea of my being possessed by another. And I had artfully (which I was convinced was in my Power) turned that dreadful Idea into the pleasing Image that my Love for, and Constancy to him, were unalterable.

I called forth all my Charms, and put in Practice all my Artifice and Cunning to bring *Herod* to my Lure, but in vain. The politic King of *Judea* would not be the Rival of one of the Masters of the Universe, who was to be the Arbiter of his Fate. To this I imputed his cold Reception of the Advances I made him; but had I once thought (what might perhaps be true) that my bold Behaviour struck him with Horror, and that his Fondness for *Mariamne* kept him constant to her, I should have despised myself for the Impotence of my own Charms: And the Moment I could have thought so meanly

meanly of myself, my disappointed Pride would have driven me to Distraction. But whatever was the Cause of *Herod*'s Coldness, his being so at all, raised in me such an inveterate Hatred towards him, that the Zeal I had against him before, for the sake of getting his Kingdom, was redoubled by the Hopes of gratifying my Revenge. However, *Herod* thought proper to wait on me to the Borders of *Egypt*, and loaded me with rich and valuable Presents before we parted; I suppose, in Expectation to have assuaged my Anger, and have made me bury his Neglect in Oblivion; but he was greatly deluded, in not considering that my Revenge was implacable.

At my Return to *Alexandria*, the first News I heard was, that *Cæsar* had made a most glorious Campaign, had conquered all *Sicily*, and forced *Sextus Pompeius* from thence: That he had reduced *Lepidus* to resign the Office, and renounce the Power and Name, of a Triumvir, and obliged him to lead a private Life: That the Senate of *Rome* strove with Emulation which should court and flatter *Cæsar* the most. But of all the Honours decreed him by the Senate, what affected me with the greatest Horror was, that they decreed a sumptuous Feast in the Capitol,

Capitol, where *Cæsar* and all his Family were to be present.

When *Anthony* returned, and I was free of *Octavia*'s Rivalship, *Livia*, *Cæsar*'s Wife, became the principal Object of my Envy. The Charms of her Person, joined to a sprightly Understanding, excited my Envy of her as a Woman; but when she became *Cæsar*'s Wife, and was to share in his Honours, my Rage against her was insupportable. She was a Woman in whose Breast Love and Ambition were so mixed, that they alternately broke forth, as Accident or outward Circumstances gave Occasion. While she lived with *Tiberius Nero*, her first Husband, and when, after the Wars of *Porus*, he wandered about, a Fugitive from his Country, her Love exerted all its Force, and she chearfully shared her Husband's Misfortunes, with the greatest Affection; but as soon as she was *Cæsar*'s Wife, as if she had been infected with a new Passion, not hitherto perceived even by herself, she was actuated by nothing but Ambition. She made *Cæsar* adopt the Children she had by *Tiberius Nero*, to the Prejudice of his own Grandchildren; and employed all her future Thoughts how to aggrandize her own Family. I was indeed pleased, that *Cæsar* had reduced *Lepidus* to a private Life;

CLEOPATRA.

Life; thinking that now the whole Power would devolve on him and *Anthony*. But yet that very Conquest which I was so pleased with, became hateful to me, when I reflected it was gained by *Livia*'s Husband, and that she was to partake in the Glory of his Victories.

Whilst my Mind was thus agitated by different Passions, and fluctuated between Hopes and Fears, a Messenger from *Anthony* arrived at *Alexandria*, by whom I was informed, that *Anthony* had made a very different Campaign from *Cæsar*. That notwithstanding he had so formidable a Power, which put all the *Indians* on the other Side of *Bactria* under the greatest Consternation, and alarmed *Asia*; yet that it proved unprofitable to him, through his impatient Desire of returning to spend the Winter with me: Which Proposal urged him to begin the War so early in the Season, and to carry it on with so little Conduct, as plainly proved to his whole Army, that he longed more to throw himself at my Feet, than to overcome the Enemy. In short, I heard that *Anthony*, after having been harrassed, and disappointed of all his Schemes, by being so far advanced in an Enemy's Country in the midst of Winter, had made one of the most miserable Retreats ever recorded in History.

History. That, what with his Retreat from *Parthia,* and marching through *Cappadocia,* amidst deep Snows, and other intolerable Hardships, he had lost above Thirty thousand of his Men; but that at last he himself was safe at the Castle of *Leucocome,* between *Berytas* and *Sidon* where he desired me to meet him, and with Impatience waited my Arrival.

Notwithstanding this News may appear so dreadful, yet I was never better pleased than at the Account of it; as in some measure it abated the uneasy Reflections *Livia* had occasioned.

'Tis true, *Cæsar* had conquered; but *Cæsar* had shewn the World that *Livia*'s Influence over him was not powerful enough to perplex him, or destroy his Conduct: Whilst *Anthony*'s whole Soul was so entirely possessed with my Image, that his Anxiety was too great for him to act with his usual Prudence.

'Tis true, *Cæsar* would let *Livia* share his Honour; but *Anthony* would venture his own Ruin, only for the sake of a more speedy Return to me. In short, on the Comparison, I thought my Glory the highest;

CLEOPATRA.

highest; and believe I was better satisfied, than if *Anthony* had carried on the War with more Succefs, had wintered his Troops in *Armenia*, and shewn the World he could bear my Absence; even though the Refult of his Succefs had been his returning home crowned with Conqueft. For though Avarice and Ambition both united in my Defire of *Anthony's* gaining new Kingdoms, becaufe I knew he would lay them at my Feet; yet his being my Slave, and the World's feeing he was the Dupe of his Paffion for me, were my principal Points in view.

Anthony's Meffenger took an Opportunity to enlarge on his Mafter's Praifes; informing me, that whilft his Soldiers were in all the Mifery which the greateft Hardfhips, the moft diftreffing Want, and the utmoft Danger could bring, he became a Father to them; ran from Tent to Tent; procured Relief for the Sick and Wounded; and with his own Hands adminifter'd to their Neceffities, whilft Tears fhewed the Tendernefs of his Compaffion. No doubt but the Meffenger imagined thefe his Praifes of my Lover would afford me much Pleafure; but he was miftaken; for I did not want to be informed, that *Anthony*, when no other Paffion intervened to get the better of it, had naturally a great

Fund

Fund of Humanity in his Bosom; but from the Time I knew him, it had been my chief Care to stifle all Sensibility to the Sufferings of others, and make him believe there was no Object of Compassion, no proper Person on whom he could exert his Goodness, besides myself; so that when I heard of his Kindness and Benevolence to his Soldiers, I thought myself deprived of my Due; and nothing was so uneasy to me, as to part with any thing I imagined my Right.

I began to think now on setting forth to *Leucocome*; but before I had left *Alexandria*, another Messenger arrived from *Anthony*, who desired me to make haste to his Lord; for that his Impatience to see me had made him like one frantic: That, in order to shorten the Time, he gave himself up to Drinking and Voluptuousness: That he could not even bear the Tediousness of a Meal; but often ran to the Sea-side, to discern if I was coming. To which the Messenger added, that he believed, if I did not appear very soon at the Castle, *Anthony*, through Impatience, would dispatch all his Attendants, one after another, to fetch me, and be left there by himself.

Nothing

Nothing could give me more Satisfaction than this Defcription concerning *Anthony*. However, the more I heard of his Uneafinefs at my Abfence, the longer I delayed gratifying him by my Prefence; for nothing could divert me fo much as the Number of Meffengers I met in my Way; and I pictured to myfelf every Hour, *Anthony* playing fome mad Prank, and making himfelf ridiculous on my account. I had often indulged the Foible of my Sex, in keeping favourite Monkies, and had always been diverted with them, in proportion as they fawned upon me, whilft they fcratched and bit every other Perfon that approached them; but the having it in my Power thus to make a Man, a *Roman* General, one of the Three Lords of the Univerfe, a Monkey for my fake, was fuch exulting Pleafure, fuch rapturous Joy, as is not to be defcribed. And what ftill added more to it was, the Reflection that *Anthony*'s Underftanding was allowed to be fuperior to that of moft other Men.

This highly delighted me, as it flattered the Conceit of my own Power, in gaining fuch Afcendency over a Perfon of *Anthony*'s Senfe and accomplifhed Abilities. Here alfo another Comparifon with *Livia*, wherein I imagined myfelf to have greatly the

Advan

Advantage, occurred to my Mind. *Livia* had indeed in *Cæsar* a fond and indulgent Lover; but yet her Power did not extend so far as to alter his Nature, or infatuate his Reason. No---such Triumph was reserved for *Cleopatra* only; and I believe no Woman could have enjoyed the Triumph more.

This Phrenzy of *Anthony*'s lasted till I came into the Port; when he broke forth into the utmost Transports of Joy imaginable. I had brought with me some Cloathing, and small Presents, for his Soldiers: But *Anthony* was profuse in his Generosity toward them; which he took care to attribute to my Liberality, and contrived that I should have the Honour of it: Though indeed the Money issued from his own Coffers; for I never parted with any thing more than I was persuaded I should, in some shape or other, receive Interest for, even to Extortion.

Anthony, by my Advice, in the Letter he wrote to the *Roman* Senate, put false Colours on the disadvantageous Campaign he had made. For though I knew common Report would discover the Truth, yet I thought a little Deceit would do no Harm.

Though *Cæsar* underhand loved to spread these Reports, yet he ordered Supplications and Thanks to be given to the Gods for *Anthony*'s Success. I saw this was setting Deceit against Deceit, which I imputed to the Artifices of *Livia* and *Octavia*. For *Octavia* had been all this Time in *Rome*; but now being desirous to seek her Husband, she obtained her Brother's Permission for that Purpose.

Cæsar was very ready to consent; thinking if *Octavia* was treated with Indignity, it would be a good Pretence for a civil War. He sent by her very magnificent Presents to *Anthony*. Nothing could be so terrible to me as the Thoughts of *Octavia* and *Anthony*'s meeting. She had already had the Power of detaining him from me Five Years; and I dreaded the Consequence of her seeing him again. I therefore took care to contrive that she should receive Letters from *Anthony*, signifying his Pleasure that she should wait for him at *Athens*; assigning for an Apology, the troublesome Wars wherein he was now engaged, which, he said, would not permit him to enjoy her Company at present. *Octavia* could not be ignorant whence these Orders of her Husband proceeded; yet she sent him Letters full of Respect and Affection, desiring to know how he would have the Provision she had made for his Use be disposed

posed of. For she brought with her Clothes for his Soldiers, Horses, Money, and Presents to his Friends and Officers, and Two thousand chosen Soldiers to recruit the *Pretorian* Cohorts he had lost. *Niger*, one of *Anthony*'s particular Friends, was entrusted with this Commission; who, after having given *Anthony* full Information of what he had in Charge, closed it with great Commendations of *Octavia*; in which I joined to so extravagant a Degree, that I could plainly perceive, I rather fixed *Anthony*'s Thoughts on my Goodness, (who could thus praise a Rival) than on *Octavia*. But I took care to throw in now-and-then, as one of her good Qualities, that she was *Cæsar*'s, the powerful *Cæsar*'s, Sister: Which I saw dwelt so strongly on *Anthony*'s Mind, as in that One Qualification all her good ones were passed over and forgotten.

I knew *Octavia*'s Design in quitting *Rome,* was to lay in her Claim, and contend with me, for her Husband's Affections; which I thought was so very unreasonable, that I resolved on no Account to be separated from *Anthony,* whose present Purpose was to join with the King of *Media* once more to take the Field against the *Parthians.* But my Design was far otherwise; for the Suspicion, that when *Anthony* approached *Athens,* he might take a Fancy to visit his

his Wife, was so shocking to me, that I displayed all my Art, and set to work all the Cunning which Experience and a strong Desire of deceiving could inspire me with, to prevent this dreadful Interview. In order to keep *Anthony* from pursuing his own Schemes of going into *Parthia*, I pretended to be dying for Love of him. By Fasting, and every Invention I could suggest, I brought myself down to be so thin, and look so pale and wan, that I seemed to be consuming away with Pensiveness and Sorrow. Whenever he entered the Room, I fixed my Eyes on him with Rapture; and whenever he took his Leave, I was fainting and dying away. I saw this worked *Anthony* into Agonies, and he would often run from me, as unable to support my Sufferings. But the Moment he departed, I burst out a laughing at his Folly, and exulted in the Superiority of my Power.

Whenever he left me in this Condition, he was expeditious in his Return; for he was equally unable to bear the Thoughts of what I might suffer, as to be a Witness of it. I had acquired the Art of appearing in Tears at a Moment's Warning; but as soon as he approached, I affected to dry them up in Haste, as if ashamed he should be a Witness of my Confusion and Disorder; or rather, as if unwilling to grieve him, I would endeavour, if possible, to keep all my Sorrow to myself. Nay, sometimes the very Tears which had started into my Eyes with Excess of Mirth and Laughter in his Absence, would serve to persuade him that they flowed from a quite different Motive.

I had hitherto pleased myself with imposing so grosly on *Anthony*, as to make him believe all the Marks of other Passions, such as Anger, Pride, and Envy, were Marks of Love. This I delighted in most, as I fansied my Power raised in Proportion to the Grossness of my Imposition. But now, imagining that if he went to the *Parthian* War, *Octavia* laid in wait at *Athens*, to seduce him from me, I thought it proper to come nearer the true Signs of Love in outward Appearance, in order to prevent his being thus seduced.

Anthony was at present so surrounded and beset with my Creatures and Flatterers, who were all so zealous to second my Design, that he heard from them nothing but the Words I had dictated, and the Sentiments which I chose he should be inspired with. They loaded *Anthony* with Reproaches: They charged him with Insensibility, and upbraided him with

forcing

forcing an unhappy Lady to die for his fake; a Lady, whofe Soul entirely depended upon him, and on him alone. They added, that it was true *Octavia* was his Wife, and did enjoy that honourable Title, becaufe it was found convenient for the Affairs of her Brother to have it fo: But *Cleopatra*, the fovereign Queen of many Nations, muft be contented with the Name of Miftrefs: Nor did fhe fhun or defpife the Character, whilft fhe might have the Happinefs of feeing and living with him. If fhe were bereaved of this, the Lofs would be too infupportable for her to expect to furvive it.

Anthony was fo well convinced that I muft die if he forfook me, and fo well fatisfied it would be an Action of great Compaffion and Goodnefs to facrifice himfelf and his Friends to *Cleopatra*, that, putting off all Thoughts at prefent of the *Parthian* War, he fuffered me to lead him back in Triumph to *Alexandria*; whilft his Wife *Octavia* waited his Commands at *Athens*, and the gazing World was aftonifhed at my Power. But notwithftanding my Triumph on this Occafion within my own Breaft, yet was I not contented without daily tormenting and plaguing *Anthony*, with exerting all the Force of the moft raging Jealoufy; bleffing in my own Mind

that

that Person who first asserted Jealousy to be one of the strongest Proofs of Love. And indeed my Fear of losing *Anthony*, (though it was on the Consideration of his being my Subject, more than my Lover) would not let me rest, whilst *Octavia* should remain quietly at *Athens*. But yet I did not dare openly to insist on his sending her rudely back to *Italy*; for my Method of accomplishing my own Purposes, was to work *Anthony*'s Passions in such a Manner, that he himself should propose the Execution of my Schemes, without my ever mentioning one Word of the Matter. However, I was resolved by some Means or other that *Octavia* should return to *Rome*. One Day, when *Anthony* was gone abroad, I indited the following Letter, in his Name, to his Wife *Octavia*.

" *Madam*,

" As the present Situation of my Affairs will not
" permit me to meet you at *Athens*, I judge it pro-
" per that you immediately return to *Rome*, till
" such time as it may be more convenient for
" me to see you either there, or at some other
" Place, which I shall take care to appoint."

This

This Letter I kept in my Pocket, till I could have an Opportunity of making my intended Use of it. *Anthony* often gave Intimations as if he wished *Octavia* was returned to *Italy*; and I was resolved, the next Time I found him in that Humour, to bring it about. It was not long before he mentioned his Wife, when I repeated my former extravagant Praises of her; concluding again with her being *Cæsar*'s Sister. *Anthony* changed Colour; looked angry; and said, he would send her back to *Rome*, if it was only to shew *Cæsar* he defied his Power. In Appearance I was very much against such a Proposal; and replied, it would be dangerous to irritate *Cæsar*, by so public an Affront offered his Sister. I urged all the Reasons I could against it, till I saw he was inclinable to be prevailed on by my Arguments; and then I suddenly concluded with begging him to remember what the Astrologer had formerly told him; and, for his own sake, to dread the Wrath of him whose Genius was the stronger, and which awed his into Fear and Trembling. This answered my Purpose; for *Anthony* fell into a violent Rage; repeated the Words, Fear and Trembling, several Times; and then broke out into such Expressions, as plainly shewed he was determined *Octavia* should not hold him by Fear, nor would
he

he be terrified by *Cæsar*'s Wrath. As soon as his Rage was abated enough to hear me speak, I told him, with a smiling Countenance, that he, I was confident, would not send a Letter of my dictating to *Octavia*, to command her to return to *Italy:* And, as soon as I had dared him into swearing he would send whatever I indited, I left him, with a Pretence of writing the Letter, and I brought him that above recited. As soon as he had read it, he took the Pen to copy it, which I with great Eagerness dissuaded him from. I assured him it would bring on a civil War: That it was impossible *Octavia* could brook such an Affront; and many more Arguments I used, all of which tended to spur him on to put in Execution what I affected to desire to prevent. At last, when I knew he was possessed with the Sort of Spirit my Letter contained, I snatched it away from him, and burnt it; saying, what I had done only through Pleasantry, and in Jest, should not be the Cause of his venturing to displease *Cæsar*. Thus I thoroughly convinced him of my affectionate Concern for his Welfare, whilst I urged him on to the gratifying my Wish, to Appearance against my Will.

The Letter he sent was (by means of the Humour I had put him into) more insolent, and fuller

of

of Contempt, than that I had indited. *Octavia*, always obedient to her Husband's Commands, immediately returned to *Rome*; whilst I again triumphed in the Success of my Schemes, and in my extensive Power over *Anthony*.

Sextus Pompeius, after he was driven by *Cæsar* from *Sicily*, had endeavoured to attach himself again to *Anthony*; but at the same time, apprehending this Attempt would be unsuccesful, he had sent Ambassadors to the King of *Parthia*, that at all Hazards he might secure himself a Refuge. This was discovered to the Triumvir; and Ambassadors were dispatched from *Pompey* to *Alexandria*, to excuse his Treachery by the Necessity of his Circumstances, and to obtain his Pardon of *Anthony*. I seconded *Pompey*'s Petition with all my Might; not that the Remembrance of his Brother gave me any Inclination to preserve his Family: For an Inclination to serve others, unless I was to be the chief Gainer by it, was a Guest to which my Bosom was an utter Stranger. But my real Motive to follicit for *Pompey* was, that notwithstanding I had now sent *Octavia* far from *Anthony*, yet I thought it possible they might one Day be re-united; and in that Case, I was in hopes by my Arts to allure *Pompey* to supply

R *Anthony*'s

Anthony's Place; and by our joint Forces, and his Valour, that he might become even *Cæsar*'s Rival. But *Pompey* still continuing his double Dealing with *Anthony*, fell afterwards into the Hands of *Titius*, who had a personal Pique against him; and therefore, by a pretended Mistake of *Anthony*'s Orders, put him to Death; which put an End to all Designs against him; and I was obliged to turn my anxious and restless Thoughts to the Production of some new Scheme or Project.

When *Anthony* last conducted his Army into *Parthia*, *Artabazes*, King of *Armenia*, who pretended to be his faithful Ally, by withdrawing his Troops from his Assistance, was the principal Cause of the Triumvir's Misfortunes. This harboured in my Mind; for I was as implacable in my Revenge as insatiable in my Avarice. The former I intended to satisfy in the Destruction of *Artabazes*; and the latter, in the Possession of his Kingdom. Revenge was so pleasing and delightful to me, that I was glad to indulge it on *Anthony*'s Enemies, where my own Interest was not concerned, and I had not acted in Concert with them. *Octavia* being now returned to *Rome*, I thought it a proper Season for *Anthony* to obtain Possession of *Armenia* himself, and to bring
Artabazes

Artabazes into his Power; which I advised him to effect by Force or Treachery, Menaces or Promises, or by any Means most likely to succeed his Purpose. Whilst *Anthony* was absent, I was greatly perplexed in my Thoughts with the News I heard of *Cæsar*; namely, that he had led his Forces into *Illyria*; had made great Conquests there, and carried the Glory of the *Roman* Army where yet the *Roman* Name had not been heard. But what chiefly moved my Indignation, and roused all the Venom I had nourished in my Bosom to sting and gall me, was *Cæsar*'s building, with the Money he had raised in *Illyria*, a magnificent Portico, which he consecrated to *Octavia*'s Honour, and which he called by her Name. There he placed the Standard he had taken from the Enemy; and the Statues and Pictures with which it was ornamented, were of an inestimable Value.

I had so long been accustomed to imagine myself a Loser by whatever Good others enjoyed, or whatever Honour they attained, that, if possible, I would have amassed to myself all the Treasure, and grasped all the Power, the World contained. But when I considered, that these Treasures and this Glory were to be shared by my Rival, it overwhelmed me with

Envy, and filled my Soul with the moſt horrible Deſigns which the moſt implacable Hatred could inſpire. Beſides, *Octavia*'s Behaviour ſo far heightened my Grief, as to tranſport me almoſt to Madneſs. For on her Return from *Athens*, *Cæſar* would have prevailed on her to quit her Huſband's Houſe, in Reſentment of his injurious Treatment, and to return home to him. But ſo fixed was her Reſolution, that no Injury offered her by *Anthony* ſhould provoke her to move One Step without his Commands, that ſhe, in Oppoſition to all Perſuaſions, continued in his Houſe; where her conſtant Employment was not only the Care of her own Children, but likewiſe thoſe which *Anthony* formerly had by *Fulvia*, excepting the Eldeſt, who was with his Father. All *Anthony*'s Friends, who had any Pretenſions to Preferment, or came to *Rome* upon private Buſineſs, ſhe received very kindly, and preferred their Petitions to *Cæſar*. This Deportment juſtly gained *Octavia* the Eſteem and Love of the judicious Part of Mankind. It was very ſurpriſing that my Rival's Goodneſs ſhould create me ſo much Uneaſineſs, whilſt I flattered myſelf that I deſpiſed it as Meanneſs of Spirit: But now I am ſenſible the true Reaſon was, that the Force of Truth irreſiſtibly ſtruck on my Mind, and that my inward Approbation of *Octavia*'s Conduct

was

was one of those Actions, which, by the Help of a strong Imagination, we artfully conceal from ourselves. But this inward Approbation of *Octavia* incensed my Rage against her to such a Degree, that I resolved to set the World on Fire, sooner than she should enjoy even that Retirement she seemed to chuse, upon her Husband's Neglect and Scorn.

I wrote to *Anthony* at all Events to hasten his Return; and if he could not get *Artabazes* either by Treachery or Force into his Power, to delay the Execution of that Design to another Season; for I could no longer support his Absence. As soon as I saw him, it was my Intention to kindle a civil War between him and *Cæsar*; in which he must either become Master of the World, and make me Mistress of the *Roman* Capitol, or fall in the Attempt.

I warmed my Imagination, and indulged my Fancy to such an Excess, in the Thoughts that I should, by *Anthony*'s Means, become Mistress of the World, that I could set whole Hours and entertain myself with the Prospect of being at the Capitol of *Rome*, assisting there at a solemn Festival instituted to *Anthony*'s Honour, after his Conquest of *Cæsar*. What made this take such strong Possession of my

Thoughts,

Thoughts, was the Pain I suffered in the Reflection, that *Livia* and *Octavia*, as Wife and Sister to *Cæsar*, had been admitted to that Honour. Nay, I proceeded so far, as to form Speeches in my Mind to vex those Two Objects of my Envy, and consequently of my most inveterate Hatred; in which, I am very certain, no One Instance of Insult, Spite, or Malice, was omitted. Sometimes I even spoke these Speeches aloud, as if the Persons to whom they were intended to be addressed were present; when I practised all the malicious Sneers, and scornful Gestures, that could possibly be produced by the most consummate Pride, or wanton Insolence. The Strength of my Imagination, by assisting to place before my Eyes these charming Pictures of what I would do when I was Mistress of the World, was the Cause of all my future Misfortunes; for I was so wrapt in these Thoughts, that the human Mind being too narrow to conceive many Ideas at one and the same time, I made nothing further my Point than the securing *Anthony* from escaping my Power; taking it for granted, that every thing else would follow to my Wish; which made me often destroy my own Purposes, and act in such a manner, as prevented the Success of my own Schemes.

Anthony

Anthony obeyed my Summons, and haftened his Return. He had purfued my Advice, in laying afide all Scruples that might have withheld him from Treachery; for by fair Promifes, and the moft folemn Engagements of his Word, for *Artabazes*'s Safety, he had allured the deluded Prince to refign himfelf to his Power; when he immediately loaded him with Chains, and brought him a Prifoner, with his Wife and Children, to *Alexandria*. I was inexpreffibly rejoiced to meet my Hero victorious; for fo I called him; although his Spoils and Prifoners were indeed the Production of Perfidy, rather than of Conqueft.

Anthony entered the City in a triumphal Chariot, caufing the Spoil he had taken in *Armenia*, with King *Artabazes*, his Queen, the Prince and Princeffes his Children, with other Prifoners, to be carried before him in the fame manner as was cuftomary in the Triumphs at *Rome*; only with a Difference which to me was very effential: For whereas at *Rome* the Proceffion ended at the Temple of *Jupiter* in the Capitol, here it ended at the Perfon of *Cleopatra*; for I took the Place of the God, and was feated in public on a golden Throne, placed on a Scaffold,
overlaid

overlaid with Silver, and surrounded by the People on every Side.

When *Artabazes* and the other Prisoners were presented to me in Chains, I expected they should have kneeled down before me; and my Flatterers pressed them much to pay me that Adoration; but they too well remembered their former Dignity to comply with so low and mean a Submission. This Refusal of theirs cost them very dear; for I had no Notion that any Mortal should presume to imagine he could attain to any higher Honour than that of being my Slave; and so enchanted was I with Pride, that I had an Inclination to keep it entirely to myself: For which Reason I was determined to punish any Person severely, who had the Insolence to be my Rival; and therefore I took care to have these audacious Prisoners treated afterwards as I thought they deserved, for daring to suspect I was not a real Goddess.

A little time after this Triumph, *Anthony* having feasted the People of *Alexandria*, called them together in the Place of public Exercise; where, being seated on a Throne of Gold, and placing me in another, he declared *Cæsarion*, my Son by *Julius Cæsar*,

CLEOPATRA. 129

Cæsar, in Conjunction with me, to be King of *Egypt* and *Cyprus*; and whereas I had brought him Three Children, to *Alexander* he gave *Armenia*, *Media*, *Parthia*, and the rest of the Eastern Countries from the *Euphrates* unto *India*, where they should be subdued. To *Cleopatra*, the Twin Sister of *Alexander*, he gave *Lybia* and *Cyrene*; and on his youngest Son, whom he surnamed *Philadelphus*, he bestowed *Phenicia*, *Syria*, *Cilicia*, and all the Countries of the lesser *Asia* from the *Euphrates* to the *Hellespont*; and conferred on each of them the Title of KING of KINGS. He gave me the Name of *Isis*, whilst he assumed to himself that of *Osiris*: The first was the great Goddess, and the other the great God, of the *Egyptians*. From this Time we both frequently appeared in public, habited in the Dresses which were then appropriated to those Deities. *Anthony* also in an Oration, wherein he, with all the Eloquence he was Master of, exaggerated my Praises, declared I was Wife to *Julius Cæsar*, and consequently that *Cæsarion* was his lawful Son.

In the midst of these Honours paid my Children, *Anthony*'s eldest Son by *Fulvia*, then with him, was taken no Notice of. I had engaged *Anthony* to send for this Son from *Octavia*, and intended to get the rest

rest of *Fulvia*'s Children from her, for Two Reasons. First I envied the Goodness of her Behaviour towards them; and secondly, I had a mind to have them in my Power, that my own Children might insult them. For as I had no Love for *Anthony*, but only looked on him as a proper Object to gratify my Pride, by his being my Slave, I hated those Children he had by any other Woman, as they brought to my Remembrance the uneasy Reflection, that another Woman had once as great an Influence over him, as *Cleopatra* now had. Besides, I thought the getting his Children into my Power, would still be another Argument to the World, how intirely I governed him; and though I had so many and such strong Proofs of my unlimited Sway, yet would I not forego the minutest Trifle, which I could by any means put into that Scale of my Happiness. And although I said I wanted *Fulvia*'s Children only that mine might insult them, yet I had no Fondness even for my own, as indeed the suffering them to insult others sufficiently proved; but I imagined that the keeping up the Dignity of what was my own reflected back on myself; and I believe no one Woman was ever more enamoured with her own Dignity and Power.

The

The Order of the Triumph, *Anthony*'s Gifts to my Children, and, in short, all the Transactions I have now related, were the Effects of my Cunning and Contrivance. But was I to repeat particularly every Art I made use of to work *Anthony* to my Purpose, Ages would not suffice to relate the History of my Life; for as quick as Thought, new Tricks and new Forms of Deceit presented themselves to my Mind; and the Execution always kept Pace with, and immediately followed them.

I was sensible what Murmurs *Anthony*'s Behaviour would create in *Rome*, and that the politic *Cæsar* would take every Advantage against him; and likewise that the Acknowlegement of *Cæsarion* to be the legitimate Son of *Julius Cæsar*, must irritate *Octavius* to the highest Rage; as it was raising him a Rival in the Empire in the lawful Heir of the Dictator; but this was my Design. For as my Purpose was at all Events to drive on a civil War, the more incurable the Breach was between *Anthony* and *Cæsar*, the more it contributed to my principal View.

But in the midst of the various Reflections that possessed me, and whilst my only Delight was placed in the Hopes of gratifying my Ambition, I was

was obliged not to forget *Anthony*'s Pleasures; for the Moment I gave him Time to free his Mind, and rouse himself from the Love of his Pleasures, I knew I must lose him. We therefore continued revelling and feasting as before; and I had the Art, at Intervals, when I found it necessary for my Purpose, to lay aside all my Cares, and employ all my Thoughts in Endeavours to enhance *Anthony*'s Gratifications. One Evening, when *Anthony* had provided a very expensive Supper, I told him in a Vein of Pleasantry, that his whole Entertainment was trifling in Comparison of what I could do; for I would provide him a Supper in which we might each of us consume more than the Value of Six Million Sesterces. I continued jesting with him in this Manner till he looked a little displeased; and said, he would lay me a Wager I could not make good my Words. The Night was appointed, and I provided a Supper in which there was nothing extraordinary; whereupon *Anthony* fell into a Fit of Laughing, and called for the Bills that might shew what this Supper cost. I suffered him to go on, till I had worked him into the utmost good Humour; and then taking one of the Pearls out of my Ears, which was equal in Value to the Sum above-mentioned, I dissolved it in Vinegar, and drank it off. I was going to take the

other

CLEOPATRA. 133

other for *Anthony* to pledge me, when *Lucius Blancus*, who stood by, caught it out of my Hand, and declared, *Anthony* had already lost his Wager; by which means he preserved it. *Anthony* looked at first a little confounded at my Device; on which I smiling said, "these Pearls, that came into my Possession from a long Race of royal Ancestors, I would consume, as I would indeed the World itself, to give *Anthony* a Moment's Diversion." This turned him into the greatest Rapture imaginable; and he esteemed this Contrivance a Mark of my Ingenuity, and the consuming my Pearl as a Sign of my Love. But I took care to have that Expence amply compensated by the Profusion his extravagant Fondness for me produced.

We now set Sail for *Ephesus*; where *Anthony* ordered the Rendezvous of his Fleet, which consisted, including the Tenders, of Eight hundred Vessels, whereof I furnished Two hundred with Twenty thousand Talents, and Provision for the whole Army, during the War. *Anthony* was advised by his best Friends to send me back into *Egypt*, there to wait the Event of the Contest between him and *Cæsar*. But this I was resolved to prevent; for I dreaded the Conclusion of another Peace by *Octavia*'s Means, much

more

more than any Defolation that could be the Confequence of purfuing the War. I bribed *Canidius*, therefore, to plead my Caufe with *Anthony*, and to lay before him how unjuft it was, that One who bore fo great a Share in the Charge of the Expedition, fhould be debarred her Share of the Glory; and alfo, how unpolitic it was to difoblige the *Egyptians*, who made fo confiderable a Part of his Naval Force; concluding with his Commendations of my Prudence and good Senfe, in my Government of a great Kingdom by myfelf alone. I placed myfelf where I could over-hear what *Canidius* faid; and entered the Room juft as he finifhed his Harangue, as if I had only heard the laft Words. I ran up to *Anthony*, looked at him with a languifhing Softnefs, and then cried out, " Oh! *Canidius*! name not the Time " when I ruled without my *Anthony*; for I would, " if poffible, forget every Moment of my Life when " he was abfent." The amorous *Anthony*, eafily invited to follow his Inclinations, gave Way to my Defire; and we failed together for *Samos*. Here all the Kings, Commonwealths, and Cities that were willing to affift *Anthony*, were to bring what Provifion they had collected for his Ufe; and as I found *Anthony* was inclined at that time to be thoughtful and melancholy, which frighted me with the

horrid

horrid Idea of his being dubious concerning the War, and difpofed to Peace, I ordered Proclamation to be made, that all who delighted in Divertifement and Recreation, fhould immediately repair to *Samos*. Thus, while the other Parts were in Tears and Lamentations, this Ifland, for fome Days, was filled with all Sorts of Harmony, and the Theatre crowded with Dancers and Comedians; whilft the Kings who accompanied *Anthony*, ftrove with Emulation to furpafs each other in their magnificent Feafts and Prefents; infomuch that it was often faid, "What will they do, by way of Triumph, when they have got the Victory; fince they are at fuch an Expence of Merriment at the opening of the War?" But ftill thefe Diverfions did not perfectly cure *Anthony* of his Melancholy, which often fo deeply affected him, that he grew fufpicious of all his Attendants, as if they defigned to poifon him; and it was vifible that I myfelf was not free from his Sufpicions, for he would neither eat nor drink any thing without Tafters. But I was refolved to invent fome Contrivance to cure him of this Apprehenfion, which I at laft brought about in the Manner following. I dipped the Top of a Garland I wore on my Head into Poifon, and in the midft of our Mirth and Jollity, when the Bowl of Wine had been tafted, I

propofed

proposed the drinking our Garlands. This Proposal did not surprize *Anthony*; for it was my Custom to suggest various Whims in our Mirth, in order to heighten it. We both immediately threw our Garlands into the Bowl; but as *Anthony* was going to put it to his Mouth, I hastily stopped his Hand, and told him what I had done; adding, "I am she, my dear "*Anthony*, whom you guard against by this new Pre- "caution of Tasters. Do you think that either Occa- "sion or Invention is wanting, if I could live without you?" I then obliged a Man to drink off the Bowl, who immediately expired. *Anthony* sat for some little while in Amazement; but as soon as I read my Success in his Looks, and perceived he was softened by my Speech, I was resolved to punish him for his Suspicion of me; and fell into such a passionate Fit of Crying, as worked him into the utmost Agonies, before I would forgive him; for I intended to make him dread ever shewing the World again that I was not the Object of his Esteem. However, this Suspicion was ample Proof to me, that I retained *Anthony* entirely by his Passions; and that as soon as he was at Liberty to make the least Use of his Understanding, he would fly to *Octavia*.

From

From *Samos* we directed our Courfe to *Athens*, where I was fo jealous of the Honour *Octavia* had received (for fhe was much beloved by the *Athenians*), that I endeavoured, by all imaginable Civilities, to infinuate myfelf into their Favour. And as I was accomplifhed in the Art of pleafing, when I defired fo to do, I fucceeded fo well, that the *Athenians* decreed me public Honours, and deputed feveral of their Citizens to attend me at my Houfe. *Anthony* himfelf, who was free of that City, was at the Head of the Deputation, and chofen their Speaker. But notwithftanding their Honours, the Commendations I accidentally heard given to *Octavia* would not let me reft; and I took every Opportunity of making *Anthony* believe that his Wife's remaining in his Houfe, under Colour of taking care of his Children even by a former Wife, and of her receiving his Friends fo politely, was all done with a malicious Defign of increafing the Clamour againft him, and fpiriting up her Brother to a greater Degree of Rage. This was with One Stroke to flatter *Anthony*, and to make that Flattery fubfervient to my own Purpofe. For as his Treatment of *Octavia*, fuppofing her a good Wife, was very injurious, he was glad to acquit himfelf of that Suppofition, in order to fhew fhe deferved fuch Treatment. He fent therefore

fore an Officer to remove her from his House; which she quitted, taking with her all his Children; at the same time bursting into Tears, at the Consideration that she must be the Cause of the civil War between her Brother and Husband. She endeavoured, to the utmost of her Power, to palliate and excuse *Anthony*'s Usage of her; and would, if possible, have kept *Cæsar* from resenting it; but by my artful Trick of continually raising in *Anthony*'s Mind the Suspicion that nothing but the Fear of *Cæsar* could restore him to *Octavia*, I had rendered it impossible for her to behave in any other Manner, than what could delude *Anthony* to believe that she intended to force him back to her by her Brother's Power. I persuaded him, that her Affectation of Softness, and her Pretence of trying to calm *Cæsar*, was the Result of Art and Malice, and only practised with a View of incensing her Brother by the Thoughts of her Goodness; and that such Affectation did more Mischief than the most virulent Spirit in the World. Thus by throwing in the Words, Affectation and Pretence, I gave *Anthony* Room to imagine his Wife was the Person chiefly to blame; and I doubted not of his greedily laying hold of every Occasion to justify himself, and to keep his own Merit from sinking. No Woman, I presume, ever had a more dexterous Way of of proving her Words; for, in order to prove a violent Spirit was the only Sign of Sincerity, I, for Three or Four Days, threw myself into such continual Paſſions of Rage, as teazed and tormented *Anthony* to the very Height of what his Temper would bear; and then I ſuddenly changed the Scene, and fell into ſuch an Extravagance of Fondneſs for him, as would have convinced him of any thing I pleaſed. When I had, by theſe means, got *Octavia* out of her Huſband's Houſe, my next Step was to be revenged on all thoſe Friends of *Anthony*'s, who had adviſed the ſending me back to *Egypt* during the War; particularly *Minucius Plancus*, and *Domitius Enobarbus*, who had been moſt zealous to prevent my accompanying *Anthony* in this Expedition. As I had the Art of pleaſing to Perfection, ſo likewiſe, without uſing opprobrious Words, could I inſult and ridicule others, in ſo provoking a manner as exceeded human Patience; and by this Management I drove to *Cæſar*, all thoſe who I was reſolved ſhould not ſtay with *Anthony*, to perſuade him againſt letting my Humour have its full Career.

I had, ſome time ſince, contrived to engage *Anthony* to make a Will; in which he had confirmed to me all his Gifts; had again declared *Cæſarion* to be be the Dictator's lawful Son; and ordered, that though he died in the City of *Rome*, his Body should be carried through the Market place, and sent to his *Cleopatra*, at *Alexandria*. This Will was deposited in the Hands of the Vestal Virgins; but *Minucius Plancus*, and his Nephew *Titius*, who had signed it as Witnesses, being now enraged at my Treatment of them, revealed the Contents of it to *Cæsar*; who found Means to get it from the Vestal Virgins, and read it to the Senate; particularly marking those Places which he thought would most irritate the *Romans*. *Calvisius* also, a Dependant of *Cæsar*'s, urged other Crimes against *Anthony*; as his giving me the Library of *Pergamum*, wherein were two thousand distinct Volumes; his rising from the Table, at a solemn Feast, and making me a manifest Assignation; that he had suffered the *Ephesians* to salute me by the Name of their Queen; that frequently, at public Audiences of Kings and Princes, he had received amorous Messages from me, written in Tablets made of Onyx or Crystal, and read them openly; that when *Turnius*, a Man of great Authority and Eloquence amongst the *Romans*, was pleading, I passed by in a Chair, and *Anthony*, as one forced by the Power of Enchantment, left them in the Middle of their Cause, and waited on me home;

that

that he had given me a Guard of *Romans*, who bore on their Targets the Name of *Cleopatra*; that in all the Visits we made to the *Egyptian* Towns, I was seated in a magnificent Car, and that *Anthony* followed me on Foot, almost undistinguished from the Eunuchs of my Train; that my Oath had been for some time, " By the Right I should soon have to " command the Capitol." In short, all the ridiculous Things I made *Anthony* do, for my own Diversion, and as Proofs of my Power, were now published in the *Roman* Senate, very much to my Satisfaction; for my Design in making him guilty of so many absurd Actions, was not to conceal or secrete them: No---to those Women whose mean Spirits are actuated by the ignoble Passion of Love, I left the Desire that their Lovers should gain the Esteem and Approbation of the best and most judicious of Mankind; whilst I was actuated by the Fire of Ambition, and the Pride of exerting my Power over *Anthony* to the utmost, and then to have the Effect of that Power in his ridiculous Actions published to the whole World.

Anthony's Friends at *Rome* sent *Geminius* to let him know the State of his Affairs, and required him to be more circumspect. That he was in Danger of having

ing his Office of Conful, and all his Governments, taken from him, and of being proclaimed an Enemy to the City of *Rome*. But when *Geminius* arrived, I looked upon him as one of *Octavia*'s Spies; and therefore befet *Anthony* in fuch a manner, every Moment, that it was impoffible for any one to fpeak to him without my being prefent. At the fame time I expofed and laughed at *Geminius*, and made him the conftant Jeft of the Table, where he was always placed at the lower End. When I found that when he bore patiently all my Infults and Outrages, in hopes ftill to have a leifure Hour with *Anthony*, I threw myfelf into all Sorts of ill Temper, and would not let *Anthony* enjoy a Moment's Eafe, till he had afked *Geminius* one Night at a full Table, what had brought him thither? He anfwered, " That his Bufinefs "might very well deferve a ferious Conference. "However, one Thing he had to deliver without Re- "ferve; which was, that Affairs would wear a much "better Face, if *Cleopatra* would return into *Egypt*." I faw *Anthony* looked very much offended, but yet he was filent; and I with a fcornful Sneer replied, "You have done very well, *Geminius*, to commu- "nicate this important Secret without a Rack:" And from that Inftant it was my Study to contrive horrid

Scenes of Revenge against him. But he wisely took the first Opportunity of escaping to *Rome*; and many more of my Enemies, and *Anthony*'s Friends, were driven away by the insupportable Treatment they received from me, and my Flatterers. And now, after many Recriminations on both Sides, War was at last declared at *Rome*, in the usual Form.

The politic *Cæsar* dropped the Name of *Anthony* in that Declaration, and only named the Queen of *Egypt*. *Anthony* was now divested of his Government: For, being ruled by a Woman, *Cæsar* said, that *Cleopatra* had so bewitched *Anthony* with her Charms and Potions, that she had bereaved him of his Senses; and that it was not *Anthony* who was to manage the War against the *Romans*, but *Mardion* the Eunuch, *Photinus*, *Iras*, and *Charmian*, *Cleopatra*'s Women, who were become *Anthony*'s Counsellors, and Prime Ministers of State. *Cæsar* spoke this in Scorn; but nothing could have pleased me more, as it was, from his Mouth, a Testimony of my unlimited Power over *Anthony*, and at the same time a Sort of tacit Acknowlegement, that *Livia* could not govern *Cæsar* with the same unbounded Authority.

When

When both Sides had prepared themselves for the War, it appeared that *Cæsar* had Two hundred Gallies well equipped, Eighty thousand Foot, and above Twelve thousand Horse. *Anthony* had no less than Five hundred Gallies, equally well appointed, and most of them had Eight or Ten Banks of Oars, so very rich, as they seemed to be designed for Show and Triumph. His Land Forces were composed of a Hundred thousand Foot, and Twelve thousand Horse. He had Eleven Kings who attended him in the War. *Herod* had provided an Army for his Use; but *Malchus*, King of *Arabia*, from whom I had, by a Grant from *Anthony*, extorted that Part of his Dominions which bordered upon *Egypt*, now he found *Anthony* was involved in a War with *Cæsar*, and not at leisure to force him, refused to pay me the customary Tribute for that Part of his Dominions I had taken from him. On which Pretence I instigated *Authony* to order *Herod*, instead of assisting him, to make War upon *Malchus*. But I had a further View in this than to recover my Tribute; for I concluded, that when these Two Kings were thus set together by the Ears, one of them would be slain in the War, and then I should have his Kingdom. I hoped it would be *Herod*; against whom I entertained the greatest Hatred, for the

Reasons

Reasons I already related. *Anthony* had under his Command all that Tract of Land which lies betwixt the *Euphrates* and the *Ionian* Sea, and great Part of *Illyria*. *Cæsar*'s Government extended from *Illyria* to the Western Ocean, and from the Ocean all along the *Tuscan* and *Sicilian* Sea. As for the Division of *Africa*, *Cæsar* had all the Coast opposite to *Italy*, *Gaul*, and *Spain*; and *Anthony* the Provinces from *Cyrea* reaching up into *Ethiopia*. I shall not relate the many Letters and Embassies that passed between *Anthony* and *Cæsar*, which produced no Effect: For I was resolved to drive on the War, and make *Anthony* seat me at *Rome*, as Mistress of the Empire, or perish in the Attempt. Whilst the divided World were either engaged, or astonished Spectators of the Event of a War, wherein was to be decided the Fate of One of the Two Masters of the Universe; my Thoughts were wholly employed in the Gratification of my own Ambition, and in Prospect of being Mistress of the World, for which *Cæsar* and *Anthony* were so warmly contending.

Now drew near the famous Battle of *Actium*: *Anthony*'s Friends all endeavoured to persuade him to depend on his Land Forces, which were superior to *Cæsar*'s. Besides, his Navy was badly supplied:

His Captains, for want of Mariners, were pressing in *Greece* (which had been exhausted long before) every one they met; Carriers, Hostlers, Labourers, and even Boys; and, notwithstanding this, the Vessels had not their Complement, but remained in a very indifferent Condition for sailing. However, amidst all these Disadvantages, I was resolved *Anthony* should try his Fate, first by Sea; where if Victory was obtained, I thought I should have more Share in the Glory than at Land; as the *Egyptian* Vessels made great Part of the Fleet. Moreover, as the Time in which the Universe was to be contended for, approached, my anxious Thoughts began to represent to my Fancy, a Possibility that *Cæsar* might be the Conqueror: But then, if we fought by Land, I imagined *Cæsar* would enter *Alexandria*, and I must be taken Prisoner. Whereas, if *Anthony* was beaten at Sea, I intended to manage in such a manner, as, by a timely Flight, to make an Appearance of having betrayed *Anthony*, and by that means to secure my Peace with *Cæsar*. To try his Fortune by Land, was the Advice given *Anthony* by those Friends of his, whom I suspected of daring to wish that he would return to *Octavia*, and throw off those Chains which I had fastened on him with so much Labour and Trouble. So that the very Spirit of contradicting

dicting those I hated, weighed greatly in the Scale, and determined me for the Sea; and when once I had determined, I was resolved that my Will should not be opposed; and that *Anthony* should shew his Followers how much he was my Slave. A Sea Engagement ensued; but in the midst of the Battle, *Agrippa*, who commanded *Cæsar*'s left Squadron, extended his left Wing, with a Design to hem in his Enemy; which, when *Publicola* (who, in Conjunction with *Anthony*, commanded our right Wing) observed, he found himself obliged to take up more Room, in order to oppose and prevent *Agrippa*. This Motion made *Publicola* leave the main Body, which was much disheartened at it, and was at the same time vigorously pushed by *Arruntius*. As soon as I perceived this, though the Victory was still doubtful, and Fortune had not determined the Day; yet my Fears prevailed on me to think the worst; and being full of the Scheme of making my Peace with *Cæsar*, by betraying *Anthony*, I crouded all my Sails; flew a-cross those that were engaged; disordered *Anthony*'s Fleet by their opening and giving way to mine; and steered my Course towards *Pelloponnesus*. *Anthony*, taking with him only *Alexander* of *Syria* and *Scellius*, put himself aboard a Galley of Five Banks of Oars, and immediately followed me.

me. In the mean time, whilſt, without any Thought of him, or any Conſideration for either his Safety or his Honour, I was thinking on various Ways of addreſſing *Cæſar*, I perceived *Anthony* ſailing towards us. I was at firſt very uneaſy, and knew not which Way to ſteer. I was afraid the admitting him on board would ruin my Scheme with the Conqueror; and I had a great Inclination to refuſe it: But then I conſidered with myſelf, if *Cæſar*, though *Anthony*'s Enemy, ſhould ſtart at ſo black a Treachery, and refuſe any Commerce with a Woman who had firſt ruined, and afterwards betrayed, her Lover, that I ſhould then be loſt, without One Refuge left me to have Recourſe to for Protection. This Picture raiſed all my Fears, and moved me to ſo much Compaſſion for myſelf, that I gave the Signal to take *Anthony* on board. And now, by a ſudden Tranſition of my Thoughts, my Sorrow for *Anthony*'s having followed me was turned into Joy. For when I conſidered the numerous Spectators, who gazed aſtoniſhed at *Anthony*, whilſt he, forgetting every thing, even himſelf, had abandoned and betrayed all thoſe who were ſacrificing their Lives in his Service, only to follow my Sails; I looked on his Diſgrace as my Triumph, and exulted as much in my Imagination as if I had gained a Victory. Beſides, I ſtill flattered

tered myself, that whilst *Anthony* was so much my Slave, I need not despair of commanding the World; for I had joined those Two Ideas so strongly together, that it was very difficult to separate or disunite them. *Anthony*, without seeing or speaking to me, placed himself at the Stern, with his Head reclining in a melancholy Posture on his Hands; and thus he continued, either angry or ashamed, for Three Days, till we arrived at *Tenarus*. Here I affected a Reconciliation, by the means of my Women and others, who were Slaves to my Will. I ordered them to excite his Compassion, by strongly representing my Sorrow for what I had done, and by imputing the unfortunate Error of my Flight to the Timidity and Fears of a Woman; at the same time charging them to take occasion of intimating the Beauty and Charms of my Person, even in Grief. When they should observe *Anthony* inclined to relent and be softened, I directed them to alter their Tone, and acquaint him, that, if it was possible for me to be angry with him, how great Reason I now had to be so, when, to the rest of my heavy Misfortunes, he added the insupportable Weight of separating himself from me. In short, we were at last reconciled, on the Terms of his humbly asking Pardon for my having betrayed him, and his approaching me with the

submissive

submissive Air of an Offender, whilst I condescended to forgive him, with the Air of an offended Queen, who was wrought by Love to forget what was past, but yet who had just Cause of Complaint.

By this time several of *Anthony*'s Ships, and a great many of his Friends, who had escaped after the Defeat, were come up to him. The Account they gave of the Bravery of his Fleet, and the Fidelity of his Soldiers, who would not listen to *Cæsar*'s Ambassadors, till they were abandoned by their Officers, vexed me with the Thoughts of the Possibility of a Conquest, if I had been less hasty in my Flight. However, I could not help deriving some Consolation, from thinking such Soldiers, and such a Fleet, were deserted for my Sake.

Anthony, sorrowful and afflicted, wandered into *Africa*, attended only by Two Friends; and I returned to *Egypt*: For I now exerted all my Artifice and Cunning to get myself rid of him, instead of retaining him, as usual, with me. I concluded, that if his Ruin was inevitable, I could, by refusing him Admission, more easily make my Peace with *Cæsar*. The Fate of the great *Pompey* struck into my Mind, without giving me any Horror. The *Egyptian* Shore seemed ed to me deftined for the Grave of the *Roman* great Men, and for the freeing fucceffive *Cæfars* of their Rivals. In order to blind my Subjects, I failed into *Egypt* with Crowns on the Prows of my Ship, as if I had gained a Victory; but hearing by my Spies, whom I conftantly employed to found the Opinions of the Noblemen of *Egypt*, that feveral of them dared to think my Conquefts not worthy a Triumph, I, without any Regret, put them to Death, for fuch their Infolence and Prefumption. To increafe *Anthony*'s Afflictions, he heard that the Perfon who commanded for him in *Lybia* (to whofe Care he had committed all the Troops of that Country) was gone over to *Cæfar*. This News prompted him to put an End to his Life; but being prevented by One of his Friends, he again turned his Thoughts towards *Alexandria*. I was unwilling to receive him, now he was a Fugitive; and yet thinking the Time not ripe to deftroy him, for fear how *Cæfar* might interpret fuch an Action, I was refolved myfelf to fly from *Egypt*, and refufe *Anthony* the Comfort even of feeing me, in the Diftrefs wherein I had involved him. Between the *Red-Sea* and the *Egyptian*, lies a fmall Neck of Land, which feparates *Afia* from *Afric*, and which, in the narroweft Place, is not much above Thirty-fix Miles. I formed a

Project

Project of hauling Twenty of my Gallies over this Neck of Land, and setting them on float in the *Red-Sea*, with all my Riches on board, to seek some remote Country, where I should be free from Slavery, and where, by the Exertion of my former Artifices, I thought I might yet hope to do more Mischief, and betray more Kings or Emperors. But the first Gallies that that were carried over, being burnt by the *Arabians* of *Petra*, I desisted from my Enterprise, and gave Orders for the fortifying all the Avenues to my Kingdom. In the mean time *Anthony* arrived again at *Alexandria*; but as his Sufferings gave me no Pain, and as I was strongly possessed with the Hope of making Peace with *Cæsar*, I used all my Endeavours at present to be rid of him; and therefore treated him so coldly, and contrived so to increase the Load of Afflictions which oppressed him, as determined him to seek elsewhere that Refuge from his Misfortunes, which my Heart (ever open to receive the Successful, and always ready to exclude the Unfortunate) denied him. He therefore retired to the Sea-side, and built a House in the Isle of *Pharos*, which he called his *Timonium*; intimating thereby, that he proposed to imitate *Timon* the *Athenian*, as much in his cursing Mankind, as he was fatally like him in the Treatment he met with from his

most

most boasted Friends. Had I been sure of succeeding with *Cæsar*, he might have raved away the Remainder of his Life in this manner, without my having one Thought of even endeavouring to relieve him; but when I was informed that *Herod* had sent to *Anthony*, advising him, as the only Means of retrieving his broken Fortune, to put me to Death, and by possessing my Kingdom make Peace with *Cæsar*, and return to *Octavia*; this News revived my Envy against my Rival, and stung me with such Indignation, that I was determined to keep *Anthony* from his Wife at any Expence whatever. I therefore dispatched Messengers to *Anthony*, and by my Entreaties soon brought him back to *Alexandria*; where, apprehensive lest he should follow *Herod*'s Advice, I took care to prevent him from giving way to Reflection, by renewing our old Revels and Banquettings. We dissolved the Order of *The Inimitable Livers*, and constituted another, called *The Diers together*; which was nothing inferior to the former in Luxury and Splendor. *Anthony* was pleased with this Delusion, as it flattered him with the Notion that I was more willing to die with him, than live with any other. So far, indeed, I had serious Thoughts of dying with him, that I imagined if *Cæsar* should intend to lead me in Triumph, it would be more Glory to die with *Anthony*, than by Per-

fidiousness

fidiousness to destroy him; when that Perfidy was to produce no other Fruit, than the Contempt it deserved. However, I was resolved to be prepared against all Events; for which Reason I collected various Sorts of poisonous Drugs, in order to learn which was least painful in the Operation, by trying Experiments on such as were condemned to die. I looked on these miserable Sufferers in their utmost Agonies, with as much Calmness and Composure, as on any the most trifling Accidents of Life. But when I observed that quick Poisons occasioned sharp Pains, with frequent Convulsions, and that the milder were long a working, I examined several Sorts of venomous Creatures, and had them applied to different Persons in my Presence. Amongst them I found none comparable to the 'Asp; the Bite of which, without the least Convulsion, caused a great Heaviness in the Head, and a Propensity to Sleep; which was attended with a gentle Sweat on the Face, and such a Stupefaction, that those who were thus affected, seemed insensible of Pain, and averse to be disturbed or awakened, like those who are in a profound natural Sleep.

I ordered likewise to be built, adjoining to the Temple of *Isis*, several Tombs and Monuments, of a stupendous Height, and very considerable for the Workmanship.

Workmanship. Thither I removed my Treasures of Gold, Silver, Emeralds, Pearls, Ebony, Ivory, and Cinnamon; to all which I added prodigious Quantities of Flax and Torches. This gave *Cæsar* great Uneasiness, for fear of my immense Wealth, lest in Despair I should set Fire to and consume it, and also rob him of his Triumph. For this Reason he was daily sending Messengers, who were to feed me with Hopes of mild and gentle Treatment. *Cæsar* was yet absent; for, after *Anthony*'s Defeat, his Presence being necessary at *Rome*, the War was deferred for a Season; but the Winter being over, he hastened back to *Alexandria*, by long Marches; himself, by the Way of *Syria*, and his Lieutenants, through *Afric*. From this Time my Mind was in a State almost of Distraction. For although I had no other Consideration but the gratifying my own Ambition, yet in my immediate Circumstances, I found it almost impossible to perceive clearly what was really my Interest. Had I been sure of *Cæsar*, I had made no Scruple of giving up *Anthony*; but my Suspicion of being led in Triumph, where *Livia* and *Octavia* should behold my Dishonour, and exult in my Misery, held me still in Suspence, and undetermined what Part to act. However, we both sent Ambassadors to *Cæsar*, whilst he was in *Asia*. I petitioned

tioned for the Kingdom of *Egypt*, in favour of myself and Children; and *Anthony*, that he might live a private Man in *Egypt*; or, if that was too much, that he might retire to *Athens*. At the same time, unknown to *Anthony*, I sent *Cæsar* a golden Sceptre, Crown, and Chair. He returned *Anthony* no Answer; but promised me, there was nothing in Reason I might not expect, provided I would either murder *Anthony*, or banish him from my Dominions. I was not much shocked at this Proposition; but as I had the Art of wresting the most solemn Secrets from those who were even the most faithful, I got some Hints from *Cæsar*'s Messenger, by which I thought I had Reason to doubt his Sincerity. In this uncertain State, one Moment I pleased my Imagination with supposing *Cæsar* might yet be my Slave, and that by his Means I might triumph at *Rome* over *Livia* and *Octavia*: Then, *Anthony* was doomed to die, without any Remorse or Consideration of his Love: But again, when I recollected *Cæsar*'s Politics and Ambition, the Thought of his artful Designs, like the most pestilent Air, seized my Bosom, infected me with the most insufferable Plagues, and threw me into Agonies not to be expressed. Then were pictured again before my Eyes, *Livia* and *Octavia* rejoicing in my Misery; whilst with down-cast
Looks,

CLEOPATRA. 157

Looks I attended *Cæsar*'s triumphal Car; the gathering Multitude around, pointing me out with Scorn and Disdain, as the Woman, who by Treachery and Cunning had first ruined, and afterwards basely destroyed, *Cæsar*'s Rival in the Universe; and yet the Woman, who had not Dexterity enough to keep herself from becoming the Prey of *Cæsar*'s Power. Then would I cry out, " that sooner than " support this dreadful Image One Moment longer, " I would die Ten thousand Deaths with *Anthony*;" who happening once to enter the Apartment, just as I had pronounced those last Words, embraced me with the most passionate Fondness, and immediately dispatched another Embassy to *Cæsar*, offering to kill himself, if that would secure *Cleopatra*. Thus in the very Instant whilst I was deliberating with myself, whether or no I should be *Anthony*'s Murderer, he offered to be his own, in order to protect my Life and Safety: But yet even all this could not rouze me from fixing my Mind solely on my own Interest. *Cæsar* returned no Answer; whereupon *Anthony* dispatched in a third Embassy his Son *Antyllus* (by *Fulvia*), with a large Present of Gold, which *Cæsar* kept, without deigning to treat with *Anthony*; but to me he sent both Promises and Threats, in order to prevent me from destroying my Wealth and
Person.

Person. At last, *Cæsar* condescended to honour me with a particular Embassy, by *Thyreus*, one of his freed Men; a Man of no ordinary Parts, of a polite Address, and whose Manner was very pleasing and highly insinuating. This Ambassador was to acquaint me, that *Cæsar*, captivated with my Beauty, was as willing to be my Slave as *Anthony* himself. My Confidence in my own Charms made this Story not at all incredible; and the Raptures with which it filled my Mind, engaged me to distinguish this Person with more peculiar Marks of Respect, and to give him more frequent and longer Audiences than was customary; insomuch that *Anthony* grew jealous, and having commanded him to be whipped, sent him afterwards back to *Cæsar*. Whether *Anthony* had any other Reason for this Jealousy than my endeavouring to recommend myself to *Thyreus*, in order to prejudice *Cæsar* the more in my Favour, I could never recollect. For my Mind, fixed to a Point, and indulging itself in the agreeable Hope of making *Cæsar* my Slave, and by his means of insolently triumphing over *Livia* and *Octavia*, had no Leisure to attend to any thing beneath that glorious Ambition, and unbounded Desire of Empire. And if my Charms had any Power over *Thyreus*, he might, if he pleased, have taken the Advantage of my Resolution to comply with whatever

ever could engage him to ingratiate me with *Cæsar*, as a Woman worthy of his Love.

However, the Time was yet too premature for me to appear to *Anthony* as if I had abandoned him, left he should take Occasion from my Perfidiousness to be reconciled to *Octavia*. I therefore thought proper to make what Atonement I could for my Indiscretion, in order to allay *Anthony*'s Jealousy; and for this Purpose I expressed all the Submission imaginable. My own Birth-day I kept as was suitable to our deplorable Fortune; but his was observed with great Splendor and Magnificence. I continually intimated, that our present Fortune could not prohibit my rejoicing in the Day which gave him Birth; since however fatal might be the Event of our Loves, yet would I not but have known my *Anthony* for all the Empires of the World. *Anthony*, who did not in the least conceive that the only Truth these Words contained, was, that I would not lose the Remembrance of the Power I had exerted over him, for the sake of his being preserved from Ruin, was in such Raptures by the sudden Transition of his Mind from Jealousy and Despair, to Love and Joy, that he fell into a Profuseness exceeding all Bounds; insomuch, that many of his Guests, who sat down

in

in great Want, returned home Men of Affluence. This farther Proof, that I still held *Anthony* in Chains not to be shaken off, and that my every Word and Look were to him a supreme Command, instead of engaging me to return him one Spark of Affection, determined me to act for the future intirely in *Cæsar*'s Interest. For as it was an invariable Maxim of mine, never to do more for another than was agreeable to my own Benefit; and as I could yet make *Anthony* believe whatever I pleased to impose on him; I thought Sincerity very useless in any Transactions which passed between us. Whereas *Cæsar* was not yet in my Power; and in hopes of that happy Event, I judged it necessary to let him see I was in earnest in the Professions I made him. Thus, by acting for *Cæsar*, and imposing on the amorous *Anthony*, I expected I should secure them both; and in Pursuance of this Design, I ordered *Seleucus*, my Governor of *Pelusium*, to deliver it up to *Cæsar*. But to justify myself to *Anthony*, I gave up *Seleucus*'s Wife and Children to be punished as he commanded: And indeed I should have thought my Time but very ill employed, in the many Years I had been endeavouring to blind *Anthony*, if he could yet discern so clearly, as to know how very little it cost me to give up others to Torments, whilst those Torments

were

were any-ways conducive to the Gratification of my own Will or Pleasure.

Cæsar, as soon as in Possession of *Pelusium*, marched all his Force against *Alexandria*. *Anthony* and I now acted Two different Parts. For whilst he encouraged the Citizens to go out against *Cæsar*, I, in public, joined him, but privately forbad them to take Arms against *Cæsar*. However, on *Cæsar*'s first Arrival, *Anthony*, with Success, made a fierce Salley, routing *Cæsar*'s Horse, beat them back into their Trenches; and returning with great Satisfaction to the Palace, armed as he was, he saluted me, and recommended to my Favour a brave Soldier, who had signalized himself in that Day's Action. I, in Recompence, presented him with a Helmet and a Cuirass, all of Gold. This *Anthony* took very obligingly; for every faint Shadow of Love from me, his warm Imagination painted in the most glaring Colours: But had he known the Truth, he would have found very little Reason to have been satisfied with my Liberality on this Occasion; for I accompanied it with so winning a Grace, as pleased the Soldier much beyond the Present he received. My Experience had taught me how much it was in my Power to gain to my Side those Men, who by their Station were placed at so great a Distance from me, as prevented them from aspiring to my Love. Besides, I had a View on this Soldier, not penetrated by any but myself. As soon as *Anthony* had left me, I sent for him, and engaged him to carry *Cæsar* an Account that I intended to prevail on *Anthony* the next Day to attack him by Land and Sea; but that, by my Contrivance, both his Fleet and his Horse would resign themselves to his Power. The Soldier, won by my Smiles and Persuasions, went that Night to *Cæsar*.

Anthony had sent *Cæsar* a Challenge to fight him in single Combat; and had received an Answer, dictated by the utmost Scorn, that he might find several other Ways to end his Life. This I laid hold of to urge him on to try his Fortune against this mighty *Cæsar*, who dared to use him with such Insolence and Contempt. His Friends were astonished to see me endeavour on a sudden to rouze him from that Lethargy, wherein I had taken so much Pains to lull and stupefy him. However, such was the Force of my Importunities, that *Anthony*, now considering with himself he could not die more honourably than in Battle, resolved the next Day to attack *Cæsar* both by Land and Sea.

It

It is impossible to express the fearful Tempest which shook and terrified my Mind during that Night. Sleep fled my Eyes, and I was every Moment revolving that the next Day was to decide my Fate. Then, said I to myself, shall I perhaps be Mistress of the World, and *Cæsar*, the Conqueror of that World, shall be my Slave; or, if he deludes me, I shall be in Chains, submitting to that Yoke I prepared for the Necks of others, and which would be insupportable to my own. Should this be the cruel Fate *Cæsar* intended for me, my only Refuge was to die with *Anthony*, and to glory in the Appearance of being faithful to him; though my Life had been One continued Series of Treachery and Deceit.

At length the dreaded, and yet the wished-for, Day appeared; when *Anthony* marching his Infantry out of the City, posted them on a rising Ground, from whence he saw his Fleet making up to the Enemy. There he stood in Expectation of the Event; but as soon as ever the Fleets approached one another, his Ships saluted *Cæsar*'s; whose Fleet having returned the Compliment, they presently joined, and with all their Force rowed toward the City. *Anthony* had no sooned observed this, but his Horse deserted him in like manner, and rendered themselves to *Cæsar*;

and his Foot being defeated, he retired into the City, crying out, "That *Cleopatra* had betrayed him, " when he was fighting only for her fake." I had given Orders to fome of my moft intimate Friends, to difpatch Meffenger after Meffenger, to let me know what paffed in the Fleet and Army; for my impatient Temper could not brook Uncertainty and Delay. In the Interim my Mind fluctuated between Hopes and Fears. *Cæsar* and *Anthony* alternately took Poffeffion of my Thoughts, in exact Proportion to my Idea of the Succefs of either. But as *Cæsar*'s commanding the World was now become moft probable, my Heart feemed inclined as a faithful Companion to accompany that World he had conquered. However, when I heard that *Anthony* was raving on my Falfhood through the Streets of *Alexandria*, under Pretence of fearing *Cæsar* (though indeed it was the abandoned *Anthony*'s Defpair and Fury which I dreaded), I fled to my Monument, which I fecured as faft as poffible, that none might find Admittance without firft obtaining my Leave. I then took care to have a Report conveyed to *Anthony* that I was dead. In which Project I had a double Defign; firft, that hearing of my Death, all his Thoughts of Vengeance towards me might fubfide; and further, (as he had often, in Fits of Fondnefs, fworn he could not

not survive my Loss) I was in hopes that his Anger being mollified, by considering that my Life had been the Sacrifice of my Treachery, his Affection would again return, overwhelm him with Sorrow, and drive him on to destroy himself, whilst he would save me both the Trouble and the Infamy of such an Action. This I enjoyed with the highest Degree of Satisfaction; for I thought it was beyond Expression glorious, to make *Anthony* destroy himself for my Loss, at the very Instant he was convinced I had abandoned and betrayed him. In the mean time, a young Man, named *Cornelius Dolabella*, one of *Cæsar*'s Favourites, who had long been captivated by my Charms, and whom I had engaged to advertise me of every thing that was in Agitation, sent me Word privately, that *Cæsar*'s Reserve made it difficult to penetrate his Intentions, but advised me by all means to be on my Guard, and to suspect the worst. This Hint from *Dolabella* threw me into the utmost Consternation. It roused my Thoughts with the horrid Reflection, that, instead of the World my aspiring Ambition aimed at being Mistress of, Infamy and Scorn were like to be the Reward of my Baseness to *Anthony*. I then imediately revolved how much preferable it were to have died with him, than to suffer the dreadful Punishment which seemed now

to

to threaten and approach me. I imagined that at least I should have the Glory of being thought, by the injudicious World, to have entertained a long and constant Passion for him. The Moment I apprehended he might be further useful to me, quick as Lightning I dispatched a Messenger to inform him that *Cleopatra* yet lived for her *Anthony*, and to conduct him to the Monument. I was not afraid of his Rage; for I was perfectly assured that the Joy of thinking he should once more behold me alive, would banish from his Mind all other Considerations. But the Messenger arrived too late; for as soon as *Anthony* had been apprised of the Report of my being dead, he broke forth into this Expostulation, "Alas! "*Anthony*, what hast thou now to do in this World? "Fate has taken from thee the only Object for which "thou wouldst desire to live." He then begged *Eros*, his faithful Servant, whom he had formerly engaged in a Promise to kill him, to keep his Word, and put an End to his Master's Misery. *Eros*, shocked at such an Action, chose rather to lay violent Hands on himself, than murder his Master. Which when *Anthony* perceived, he plunged his Sword into his own Breast, and threw himself on a Couch that stood near him. The Wound, though mortal, did not immediately occasion his Death; and he was a little

recovered

recovered when my Meſſenger arrived. The Moment he underſtood that I was ſtill living, he eagerly deſired to be carried to the Door of my Monument. I would not open it, for fear of being ſurprized, but let down Cords from a Window, to which *Anthony* being faſtened, by the Help of my Two Women, who were all I truſted in the Monument, I drew him up. The Spectators, ſeeing the faint and dying *Anthony*, covered with Blood, ſtretching out his Hands to *Cleopatra*, and raiſing his Body to give us what Aſſiſtance he could, were extremely affected, and in Tears lamented his unhappy Fate. Now, likewiſe, was I, for the firſt Time, touched with Sorrow, wherein there was any Mixture of Compaſſion for the wretched *Anthony*. As ſoon as he was in the Monument, we laid him on a Bed. I ſpread my Clothes over him; ſmote my Breaſt, and tore my Hair; then wiping the Blood off his Face, I called him my Lord, my Huſband, my Emperor. In ſhort, I was mad with Exceſs of Paſſion. But if this Grief was to take on itſelf the Name of Pity, Pride, or Affectation, it would aſſume a falſe Character, for it was indeed ſuch a Compoſition of all Three, as would render it difficult to determine which was predominant. A little Compaſſion for *Anthony*, and a good deal for myſelf, overwhelmed my Eyes with

Tears

Tears of Sorrow. My Pride disappointed, in that the Object of my Power lay expiring before me, whilst I almost despaired of alluring *Cæsar*, excited my Indignation; and as I wanted Objects whereon to give it Vent, it turned its Edge on my own divided Bosom. Then recollecting, that the only Refuge left me to die with the least Shadow of Honour, was imposing on the World my violent and faithful Love for *Anthony*, in order to set forth that Love, Affectation displayed all its Extravagance, and forced me to put on a thousand theatrical Postures, which Reality and Truth would scorn to appear in. The dying *Anthony*, instead of complaining, or endeavouring to aggravate my Grief, did all he could to comfort and support me. He suppressed his Sighs; appeared chearful, and calling for some Wine, desired me not to pity him in this late Turn of Fortune, but rather to rejoice in Remembrance of his past Happiness. He advised me to take care of myself; and amongst *Cæsar*'s Friends, to apply chiefly to *Proculeius*. When he had uttered these Words, whilst his Eyes were yet fixed on mine, and with the convulsive Pangs of Death, he grasped my Hand, just as he was expiring, *Proculeius* arrived from *Cæsar*. He had heard of *Anthony*'s Death, and sent this *Proculeius* to give me Hopes of every thing from

a young

a young Hero, whose Heart was not incapable of being moved by a Lady's Charms. He was fearful of losing an immense Treasure, and likewise thought I should be no small Addition to the Ornament and Glory of his Triumph. My only Demand was, that my Kingdom might be disposed of to my Children. *Proculeius* advised me to resume my Courage, and wholly to confide in *Cæsar*. After this, *Gallus* was dispatched to confer with me a second Time; with whom I held a Conversation through a small Aperture in the Monument. He contrived to lengthen out the Conference as much as he could; and in the mean while *Proculeius*, by the Aid of a Scaling-Ladder, entered in at that Window, through which we had taken up *Anthony*. One of my Women instantly cried out, "Oh! wretched *Cleopatra*, thou art un-"done." On hearing this, I attempted to stab myself with a Dagger which hung always at my Girdle; but *Proculeius* was Time enough to prevent me; and seizing both my Hands, forced from me the Dagger, and examined my Robe, for fear any Poison should be concealed therein. After which, *Cæsar* sent *Epaphroditus*, one of his Servants, with Orders to treat me with all imaginable Gentleness and Civility; but to take particular Care that I should have no Opportunity of destroying myself.

Many Kings, and great Commanders, petitioned *Cæsar* for the Body of *Anthony*, in order to pay him his Funeral Rites; but at my earnest Sollicitation he permitted me the Honour of that Office, and gave me Leave to be as profuse as I pleased in the Expence. This Permission clearly discovered that my Wealth was no longer my own, but was to be employed according to *Cæsar*'s Pleasure and Direction.

I spared no Cost on the Occasion, but buried *Anthony* with all the Splendor and Magnificence I could devise or invent.

Soon after, this *Cæsar* himself vouchsafed to make me a Visit; which I looked on as the critical Minute wherein I was either again to re-assume my former Glory, or be lost and sunk for ever. I adorned my Chamber with various Pictures of *Julius Cæsar*; but as for myself, I had on only a thin mourning Robe, which I thought would set off the Whiteness of my Skin; and I lay on a Couch, as one destitute and forlorn. At *Cæsar*'s Entrance I arose, and flung myself at his Feet, inwardly praying that I might succeed now as when first I saw *Mark Anthony*. I called *Cæsar*, my Lord and Master. My Hair was dishevelled,

dishevelled, my Eyes bathed in Tears, my Air languishing, and my Voice trembling; which moved *Cæsar*'s Compassion to raise and lead me back to my Couch. I artfully began the Discourse on *Julius Cæsar*, and said, " It is to your great Father, Sir, I owe " the Name of Queen: From his Hands I received " the Crown. Our Love was reciprocal: If you de- " sire Proofs, here are his Letters; please to read them." Sometimes I looked passionately at the Picture of *Julius*, sometimes on his adoptive Son. " I lost you " too soon, said I (looking at the Picture of the " Dictator), O my great Protector!" Then turning my Eyes tenderly on *Octavius*, I cried out, " No! " I have found you again in another Hero, the same " as yourself; and Fate has now restored you to " me, as great and as lovely as ever." In short, I bent all the Artillery of Artifice and Dissimulation against *Cæsar*'s Breast. He looked with downcast Eyes; and as soon as I imagined I perceived the least glimmering Hope of his being staggered, I began to excuse my Conduct, from my Necessity, and the Fear of *Anthony*. But *Cæsar* interrupting me in my Justification, I had Recourse to Prayers and Tears to move his Compassion; and at the same time put into his Hands a List of all my Treasure. One of my Treasurers accused me of suppressing

many Things of Value, and reproached me for my Insincerity. I, who had been so long accustomed to be adored by all around me, could not but resent this Usage; which threw me into so violent a Passion, that I fled from my Couch, caught this impertinent Secretary by the Hair, and struck him several Blows in the Face. Besides my Passion, I had another Reason for thus suddenly starting up; which was to shew my Shape at the best Advantage to the young Hero. *Cæsar* could not help smiling at this sudden Transport, and endeavoured to pacify me. " Is it
" not very hard, mighty *Cæsar*, said I, when you do
" me the Honour of a Visit, in this my wretched
" Condition, that I should be affronted by my own
" Servants? If I have laid by any Women's Toys,
" they never were designed as Ornaments for one
" of my miserable Fortune; but that I might have
" some little Present by me to offer *Octavia* your
" Sister, and your Consort *Livia*; that by their In-
" tercession I might hope to find you in some mea-
" sure disposed to Mercy."

Cæsar was pleased to hear me talk in this Strain, being now persuaded that I was desirous to live. He therefore assured me, that whatever I had by me I might dispose of at my Discretion; and that his Usage of
me

CLEOPATRA. 173

me should be honourable beyond my Expectation. He then departed, well satisfied he had over-reached me; but he was himself deceived; for my Friend *Dolabella* found Means of again privately giving me Notice, that *Cæsar* was about to return into *Syria*, and that I and my Children were to be sent before. The Horror of being led in Triumph, pointed at, and scorned by the *Romans* in general, and in particular, of being insulted by *Livia* (which I was assured would be my Fate), tempted me to seek Death as my only Refuge; and as I now despaired of alluring *Cæsar*, I resolved, in Appearance at least, to die for *Anthony*. I therefore requested *Cæsar* that he would be pleased to permit me to make my last Oblation to his departed Brother in the Empire; which being granted, I was carried to the Place where *Anthony* was buried; and upon my Knees, accompanied by my Women, I embraced his Tomb, with Tears in my Eyes, and made over the deceased *Anthony* so loud a Lamentation, as to a right Judgment would have plainly shewn, that true Grief for his Loss did not produce such flowing Eloquence; and that all my Mourning was the Result of Affectation. In reality, I mourned for myself; but had *Cæsar* been amorous enough to have been ensnared by my Charms, *Anthony*'s

Fate

Fate might have remained for ever unlamented by the perfidious *Cleopatra*.

Having finished these Lamentations, I crowned the Tomb with Garlands, and kissing it, ordered my Bath to be prepared. After which, I sat down to Supper, and feasted sumptuously. A Country Fellow deceiving my Guards, under the Pretence of bringing me some Figs, gained Admittance, and brought me an Asp. I wrote a Letter to *Cæsar*, most earnestly entreating that I might be buried in the same Tomb with *Anthony*; for I imagined this would preserve the Appearance of my dying for Love of him. I then invited the welcome Serpent to execute its friendly Office.

But now, at the Approach of my last Hours, I could not avoid reflecting on my past Life; and found, upon the whole, that the Indulgence of my Ambition, and the cultivating in myself the Spirit of Pride and Vanity, had produced far more Misery than Happiness. How indeed can it be otherwise? when instead of restraining, we give a loose to Passions, which, like a Dropsy, increase by Indulgence, are too greedy to be satisfied, prey on our Hearts, and raise in us a Perplexity more painful than any

Misfortune

Misfortune that can attend or befal us. To be for ever pursuing what we can never attain (which is constantly the Case of ungovernable Passions), is the State of all others most to be deplored.

When in *Anthony*'s Triumph over the King of *Armenia*, I was placed on a Throne, and the Procession ended at my Feet, instead of the Statue of *Jupiter*, even whilst I was so much the Object of the public Envy, I was more grieved at observing that the Prisoners who opened their Eyes, saw I was not a real Goddess, and would not bow down before me, than I was pleased with the most extravagant Honours paid me by the deluded and enamoured Triumvir. For when my Mind was tortured by Excess of Passion, and all within was Tempest and Confusion, what Tranquility or Happiness could I possibly enjoy? But it was now too late to change this dismal Situation; and my last Minutes rolled on in the same Tumult, which had run through all the Hours of my Life preceding *Anthony*'s Death. *Cæsar*'s Power, the Triumph of *Livia* and *Octavia*, with my own approaching Fate, crouded my Mind with such various and bitter Reflections, as almost hurried me to Distraction; and at last, had I not had Art enough to impose on myself, as I had on others, and

fancy

fancy that I defpifed Life, becaufe I fixed my Thoughts on other Objects, Death would have appeared to me in its moft frightful Terrors. But I was fomewhat flattered in prefuming I fhould attain Glory by dying with *Anthony*; and by robbing *Livia* and *Octavia* (the one, my Rival with *Anthony*; the other, in the Univerfe), of their Exultation over me; and that as I could neither allure nor conquer, yet that I fhould deceive the great and powerful *Cæfar*. Thus I breathed my laft, fadly impofing on myfelf, and fell a wretched Sacrifice to that Treachery and Ambition, wherein I had fo long placed my chief Delight; and of whofe fatal Confequences I fhall be, to all future Ages, a perpetual and difgraceful Monument.

The END *of the* LIFE *of* CLEOPATRA.

THE

THE LIFE OF OCTAVIA.

HEN *Cleopatra* had finished her Story as before recited, she retired, like *Dido*, with a gloomy Countenance; and gave Place to the more pleasing Shade of the fair *Octavia*: Who approaching with a Complacence that approved her conscious Virtue, addressed herself in these mild and gentle Accents:

The Commands of the Sovereign of these lower Regions oblige me to renew my former Griefs, by recounting a faithful Narration of my Life, whilst I was an Inhabitant of the Earth.

I was the Daughter of *Caius Octavius*, by his Wife *Atia*; Persons of distinguished Rank and Virtue; and who had likewise the Honour of giving Birth to my Brother *Augustus Cæsar*. A Circumstance I the more willingly mention, in order to refute those Critics, who, from a Mistake in *Plutarch*, contend for my being descended from *Ancharia*, the first Wife of *Octavius*; and that I was therefore only Half-sister to *Augustus*.

From my Infancy, that is, from the Time I became capable of Reflection, I was taught, that to contract my Desires, to command my Passions, and to share my Pleasures with others, was the only Conduct which could promise me Happiness; and by Rules like these was all my future Life governed. My chief Care was to keep my Mind composed and undisturbed; that in every Accident which befel me, I might have Power to exert my Reason, and give my Judgment its due Scope.

As I was very handsome, and Sister to the adoptive Son of *Julius Cæsar*, I dreaded from my Youth that I should be sacrificed to political Views, and be disposed of in the solemn Tie of Matrimony to some Man, whose Ambition alone would lead him to take me as a Pledge of Friendship from the great *Cæsar*. My predominant Passion was Love; and the highest Notion I could form of Happiness, was a private Life, with a Husband who was agreeable to my Inclinations, and capable of a reciprocal Affection. But this Opinion which I had formed of Happiness with such a Husband, rendered me the more cautious of giving way to my Affections, till my Approbation of the Object made such an Indulgence reasonable. I considered with myself, that my Sentiments of a married State would not suffer me to lead a Life of Deceit or Hypocrisy; and therefore, if married at all, it was requisite for my Peace of Mind, that I should be united to a Man who was the Object of my Inclinations, and whose Disposition would make an artful Behaviour on my Part totally needless to obtain good Usage, or to secure his Esteem. I had formed and represented to myself the Character of the Man who would please me best; and resolved that (unless Considerations of State obliged me to be a Sacrifice) I would live single, if

I found it impossible to meet with the Counter-part of the Picture which dwelt in my Imagination.

But whilst I was thus amused with my own Fancies, before the civil War broke out between *Cæsar* and *Pompey*, I had like to have been married to the latter, in order to cement a Peace, and strengthen the Friendship of those Two great Men. This I must have submitted to, had my Uncle *Julius Cæsar* continued in the Opinion, that, in order to prevent the spilling of much *Roman* Blood, it was necessary to make me a Sacrifice. Nor should I in the submitting to it (whatever inward Uneasiness it had cost me) have made the least Hesitation; for I thought my private Inclinations ought not to interfere with my public Duty; nor would I have suffered them to oppose my Uncle *Julius Cæsar*'s Commands, in a Case where any Action of mine could possibly be productive either of general Peace, or universal Confusion, with all the bloody Horrors of an intestine War. But *Pompey* could by no means prove any Resemblance to the Picture in my Bosom; in which were drawn the strongest Lines of Love, and few or none of Ambition. However, by the Turn of Affairs between *Cæsar* and *Pompey*, I escaped this disagreeable Match; and my Hopes revived, that I
should

should either live unmarried, or find an Original to my beloved Picture.

There was then at *Rome* a Man of consular Dignity, named *Marcellus*, who was greatly in the public Esteem, and all those who knew him grew eloquent in his Praises. His Character pleased me much: But Fame is so often mistaken in the Motives of Men's Actions, that I could not suffer common Report to fix my Opinion, although it had Power enough to raise in me a Curiosity to be farther acquainted with the Man, whose Understanding and Goodness Fame painted in such amiable Colours. I took the first Opportunity of creating an Acquaintance with this *Marcellus*; and found, by the most narrow Inspection into his Conduct, that he more than answered all I had heard in his Favour; and that the Warmth of my highest Imagination could not do him Justice. In short I both liked, approved, and loved *Marcellus*. My Judgment and Inclination united in persuading me to be his Wife; and I looked on it as a particular Omen of my good Fortune, when I perceived he was destined by my Brother to be my Husband. And now I will describe to you the Picture I had long before drawn by my own Fancy.

Marcellus

Marcellus was a Person of the most worthy and valuable Accomplishments. He had an excellent Understanding, a lively Imagination, a penetrating Judgment, and was so acute in the Discernment of Things, as not to be imposed upon by outward Appearances. He could easily see through the Subtleties of Fallacy; and with the like Readiness distinguish Truth, how artfully soever disguised or misrepresented. But what was most remarkable in his Character, was the right Application he made of his superior Understanding. His Reason constantly exerted itself, and kept his Passions under such regular and due Obedience, that he was always Master of himself; and was never hurried into those Transports or Excesses, which distract the Mind, and discompose the Tranquility of human Life. His Faculties were all engaged on their proper Objects; and the usual Employments of his Time were the Discoveries of Truth, and Disquisitions of Philosophy. But then as to his Amusements, he gave way to his Imagination; loved to indulge it; and from the most trifling Circumstances could derive Pleasure and Enjoyment. This was the Cause that he was agreeably chearful amidst his deepest Studies; and could mix some kind of Instruction in the most trifling Pleasantry of his roving Fancy. For although he would

would not suffer his Imagination to take Place of his Judgment, and could plainly diftinguifh the Effects of the one from the other; yet was he not fo vainly proud of his Reafon, as to look upon the Imagination beneath the Dignity of Man; nor, in the room of that Chearfulnefs which attends a fprightly Fancy, to fubftitute a haughty Surlinefs of Temper, which of all things renders a Man moft difagreeable. Such was the Underftanding of *Marcellus*; and he thought it his Duty to enjoy the Advantages Nature had given him with a contented and a thankful Mind. Nor was the Heart of *Marcellus* any-ways inferior to his Head. He had more Compaffion in his Nature, more Tendernefs in his Difpofition, than I ever faw in any other Man. And this Compaffion, this Tendernefs, made him incapable of being guilty of any Action to which the Name of Ill-nature could properly be applied. No difdainful Arrogance, or infolent Scorn, had any Place in his gentle Bofom. The Difpofition of his Heart was as well regulated as the Faculties of his Mind. He was neither conceited enough in his own Opinion to be afhamed of Weaknefs; nor would he indulge it to fo extravagant a Height, as to fuffer himfelf to be led by it to the leaft Injuftice. When he acted in a public Capacity, he could fhed Tears for the Sufferings of thofe

whom

whom he would not relieve at the Expence of his Integrity. In short, *Marcellus* exceeded my Picture, as much as the Hand of Nature excels that of Art; and brought to my Remembrance the Story of *Pygmalion* and his Statue; for he was the Portrait I had drawn, animated with Life and Motion. To finish the whole, his Person was remarkably agreeable, his Manners were elegant and refined. As I have before observed, that Love was my predominant Passion, it would be needless to repeat how much I loved *Marcellus*. My Love was unmixed with Vanity, and my Affection free from all Considerations but the Good and Pleasure of its Object. And this Affection was so perfectly mutual, between me and my Husband, that our Thoughts were known to each other, before the Tongue could express them. *Marcellus* continually exulted in the Happiness of this Union; and often said, " That although the " married Life was what he chose, yet there was " nothing he so much dreaded as meeting with a " Wife, with whom he could not follow the natu- " ral Bent of his own Inclinations, by indulging her, " without filling her with such Affectation as would " have given him a great deal of Uneasiness. He " must then have lived in a perpetual Restraint, or " condemned himself for feeding that Vanity, which,

as

"as it is too enlarged ever to be fatisfied, muſt by "his own Fault have made the Woman miſerable, "who was intruſted to his Power." Whereas my Mind, actuated by Love only, gloried in his Tenderneſs, as a Proof of his Confidence in my Behaviour, and of his affectionate Regard to my Happineſs. Nor was I, in my great Care to oblige, and particular Caution of offending him, any-ways remiſs, in returning with Intereſt that Tenderneſs in which I ſo much delighted. His diſtinguiſhing Penetration could eaſily perceive that my Delight in his Regard for me, aroſe entirely from the Strength of my Love, and not from the common Vanity of imagining myſelf the Object of Admiration. This was the Reaſon I would not (had it been in my Power) have driven him, by his Affection for me, to have acted beneath his Character, or expoſed himſelf on my Account to Cenſure or Ridicule. Inſtead of wiſhing to have it in my Power, I was pleaſed with thinking the Foundation of my Huſband's Love was fixed on the ſteady Baſis of true Eſteem; as I knew that was the only Baſis whereon I could raiſe any ſolid Hope of its continuing firm and unalterable. *Marcellus* (had he been married to a Woman whoſe ruling Paſſion was Vanity, and who, from that Vanity, would have been unreaſonably capricious, hating his

Friends, for fear they did not respect her as much as she did herself, and making Favourites of his Enemies, in hopes they allowed her a Superiority in some shape or other over her Husband, whilst she affected an extravagant Passion for him) could not have been so deceived. Nor did his Judgment, always subtle in the Search of Truth, suffer him to run into the other Extreme; and because he knew there were many such Women in the World as I have described, deny the Possibility of any Woman's being of a different Character. Neither did he, whilst his Wife was giving him every Proof in her Power of true Respect, call it Affectation; and, by blinding himself with an imaginary Notion, indiscriminately mingle Truth with Falshood. No! *Marcellus* saw my Fidelity, and loved me for it; and his Love heightened my Affection to a Degree which, I believe, could not be exceeded. We lived together with the utmost Simplicity. Artifice and Cunning were banished our Bosoms; where there was nothing we wished to conceal; where no lurking Disguises were necessary; since mutual Confidence, Sincerity, and Truth were the constant and invariable Rules of our Conduct. In every Action of our Lives we had Reference to each other. Whether we staid at home, or went abroad, were serious or disposed to Mirth, still

still by our Sympathy and Love, every Trifle made a Pleasure, and every Pleasure was heightened into Joy by our mutual Participation of it; our Hearts exulted with that Rapture which is built on the strong Foundation of undissembled Love. Every Tree and Bush, every common Object produced by Nature, became, by our Observations, and giving way to our delighted Imaginations, Matter of the most agreeable Entertainment. Our common Friends (for we had nothing separate) rejoiced in our Company, as they were gladdened with our Happiness: For to good Minds, Happiness, like Colour to the Camelion, is chiefly communicated by that of others. My Husband's steady Understanding improved me; his Strength of Fancy entertained me; and our mutual Love, fixed on, and influenced by, Integrity of Manners, banished all tumultuous Passions from our Breasts, and left us no other Thoughts but those of Peace, Tranquility, and Joy. The public Calamity, in the Time of the famous Proscription by *Cæsar*, *Anthony*, and *Lepidus*, did indeed interrupt our Composure, move our Compassion, and fill us with Terror. What added greatly to the Horror which possessed my Mind on that Occasion, was the Consideration that my Brother was one of the chief Causes of this Scene of Slaughter and Desolation. The Vengeance

geance of irritated Enemies, the Jealousies of fantastic Women, the Fear of servile Slaves, with the Rapaciousness of the Covetous, were as so many Instruments and Ministers to execute the savage Orders for the Massacre of those unhappy Wretches, whose Names were found among the Proscribed. On the other hand, to prove the Difference of human Kind, in this general Misery were signalized some of the most heroic Acts of Fidelity and Affection. Even Slaves, habiting themselves like their Masters, met Death in their Stead: Sons, unaccustomed to disobey their Fathers, now, for the first Time, disputed their Wills, and were resolute to die the first: Women in Numbers fled, bearing their Husbands, as *Anchises* did his Father *Æneas*, on their Shoulders; with whom they secreted themselves in distant Caverns. Such Instances of Fidelity and Love were now our only Comfort, as from them alone we could imagine we were not placed amongst a Set of Animals fiercer or more cruel than Wolves and Tigers. All the Power I had I exerted to soften my Brother's Rigour. I refused my Protection to none, who could find a Method of flying to me for Refuge; and I was only grieved that my weak Efforts were in vain to stop that Effusion of *Roman* Blood, which daily presented such dreadful Spectacles to our View.

OCTAVIA.

As soon as this horrid Proscription was at an End, and my Brother *Octavius Cæsar*, with *Anthony*, and *Lepidus*, were in quiet Possession of the *Roman* Empire, I would, if permitted to follow my own Inclinations, have retired from *Rome*, and with my beloved Husband have enjoyed that Satisfaction and Tranquility, in which we both so much delighted: But my Brother, who was always best pleased when we were with him, engaged us, in Compliance with his Desires, to remain in the Metropolis. My Station unavoidably threw me into the Conversation of Women of the first Quality and Distinction; but I accounted every Moment spent in their Company as so much Loss of Time. Their Infidelity to their Husbands, and the general Profligacy of their Manners, raised in me the utmost Abhorrence of their Conduct. I often reflected with Astonishment on even the Possibility that my Youth might have been betrayed into this universal Corruption, had not the Virtue and Understanding of *Marcellus* directed my Steps, secured my Peace, and inspired me with the most steady and ardent Affection. But so precarious and uncertain is all human Happiness, that this State of Security and Pleasure could not last. For the greatest Loss which could then befal me, and that wherein all other Considerations were entirely swallowed,

now

now overwhelmed my Soul, staggered, and almost overcame the most vigorous Efforts of my strongest Resolutions. *Marcellus*, my faithful Friend, my fond Lover, and my indulgent Husband, was seized with a malignant Fever, and in the short Space of Two Days his Physicians declared there were no Hopes of his Recovery. He kept his Senses to the last, and in his expiring Moments acknowledged my Faithfulness and Truth; but begged me, as soon as possible, to calm my Mind, and to consider, that the only remaining Proof I could give of my Love towards him, was to struggle with the Grief he was sensible must at first pierce my Heart; and to turn all my Tenderness on his Offspring; the dear little Pledges of our constant Passion. "So far am I,
" continued that great and good Man, from selfishly
" desiring the Remembrance of me should be the
" Occasion of your Sorrow, that nothing could now
" be so real a Comfort to my Thoughts, as the hav-
" ing any Hopes you might ever enjoy with another
" Husband, that Happiness which I have made it the
" Study and Pleasure of my Life you should partake
" with me. Perhaps your Station may demand
" your Hand as a Sacrifice to the public Peace. If
" so, your own Goodness, my *Octavia*, will direct
" you how to act; and I am satisfied my Advice
" would

"would be unneceffary and ufelefs. But turn from me the tender Softnefs of your Eyes; and remember it is my dying Requeft, that you endeavour, with all your Strength, to furmount your Affliction for my Lofs." In Words like thefe, which in broken Accents forced their Way from his trembling Lips, my dear *Marcellus* breathed his laft, and left me in Appearance dead as himfelf. My Grief, which was too intenfe for Utterance, too deep to vent itfelf in Words, flew to my labouring Heart, and, for the prefent, deprived me of Life and Motion. My Attendants took me from this difmal Scene, and bore me to an Apartment far diftant from my deceafed Hufband. There I lay fome Hours, as in a Trance; but yet my Imagination bufied itfelf in confufed and wretched Ideas. One Moment, flufhed on my too faithful Memory all the paft Scenes of Tendernefs I had enjoyed with my late *Marcellus*. This forced Tears from my Eyes, till they could flow no longer; and the direful Thought that he was dead, and I fhould never behold him again, tortured my Soul. His uncommon Generofity, in fo earneftly wifhing my Happinefs, when he himfelf fhould be no more capable of fharing it, raifed my Admiration, and increafed my Grief.

In this Agony of Sorrow I formed no Resolutions of not marrying again. My Soul was so entirely fixed on my irreparable Loss, that there was no Room for even the Thoughts of a second Husband to find a Place in my distracted Mind. But when, by the Abundance of my Tears, and the long Roving of my bewildered Imagination, my Misery was a little exhausted, and consequently began to subside; I reflected, that it was the last Command of *Marcellus*, that I should struggle to surmount my Affliction, in order to shew him the only remaining Testimony of my Love, by my tender Care of our Offspring. This excited my Attention; and I cried out, " Shall then " the dying Command of my beloved Husband be " the only one in which I ever disobeyed him? Is " there any the most trying Proof of Regard I would " not grant him? Shall *Octavia* give a Loose to " Sorrows (which, as they are the present Bent of " her Nature, would be her greatest Indulgence) " till they sink her to the Grave? And shall she " want Courage to live, in order to preserve all the " dear Remains of *Marcellus* from being tossed, help- " less and forlorn, on this merciless and unrelenting World? This Consideration had Force enough to enable me to exert my utmost Strength to assail my Grief, and prevent its preying too deeply on my Heart.

However,

However, I could not conquer my Sorrow so absolutely, but that for Hours and Days it would be my wretched Companion; although by my outward Behaviour, and often by my chearful Countenance, it was generally believed no Woman could be less concerned for her Husband than myself. My real Trouble was so great, that had I not kept it under due Moderation, it must have inevitably terminated in my Death; whereas those Sorrows, with which we are but slightly affected, may break forth, and be again restrained, at our own Will or Pleasure, and according to the outward Appearance we think most proper to make.

By my Brother's Consent, I now retired a little while from *Rome*; and in this Retirement I intended to pass the Residue of my Days, employing myself in a careful Education of those dear Infants for whose Good alone Life was any longer desirable, or the Object of my Wishes. But, alas! this was not allowed me. I was destined to appear again on the public Stage; and the Part allotted me was both difficult and painful to perform. A civil War was already broke forth between *Cæsar* and *Anthony*. But *Fulvia*, *Anthony*'s Wife, who, to force her Husband from *Cleopatra*, had been the chief Promoter of this War, being now dead,

dead, the common Friends of the Two Triumvirs proposed the giving me to *Anthony*, as a Pledge of Peace, and a Means of future Union between them. When *Cæsar* sent me this Proposal, I was shocked much more than if he had decreed my Death as the Means of the public Good. A retired and solitary Life with my late Husband's Offspring was all the Comfort my irreparable Loss had left me. The Name of Wife, once so much my Glory, and my Joy, was now to become my Misery; and instead of *Marcellus*, I was to call *Mark Anthony* by the once-loved Name of Husband. I could form no Conception how it was possible for me to live with him; as he had been the Dupe both of *Fulvia* and *Cleopatra*. *Fulvia*, whilst *Anthony* was Master at *Rome*, after the Death of *Julius Cæsar*, had made all Things venal, and in her own Apartment, sold Governments, Provinces, and Kingdoms, to the best Purchaser. She was not ashamed to bear the Sword to head the Senators of her Party; to harangue, and give Orders to the Soldiers; and mix in Council with the Generals. During the dreadful Proscription before-mentioned, she herself, from private Pique, and implacable Revenge, commanded the Massacre of several Men whom the Triumvirs had spared. Even beyond the Grave did her Revenge pursue

purſue her Enemies. For when the Head of *Cicero* was brought her, taunting, ſpitting on, and inſulting it, ſhe pierced his Tongue ſeveral Times through with a Bodkin, and lamented his being dead, only as it was out of the Power of her Malice to murder him over again. And as to *Cleopatra*, ſhe ſcrupled no Murder, Treachery, or Artifice, to gratify her Ambition, and indulge her extravagant Humour. What Hopes then could I entertain, but that the Man, who had been Slave to Two ſuch Women, would deſpiſe and ſcorn a Wife of a quite different Character? What Reaſon had I to believe but that he would call Meekneſs, Meanneſs of Spirit? and think a Diſpoſition inclined to forgive, was only owing to a Want of Reſolution, and a wavering unſteady Temper? *Fulvia* and *Cleopatra* had ruled him by Stratagem and double Deſigns; I had never an Intention in any one Action of my Life beyond what I openly avowed to my Friends. I had from my Infancy contracted the utmoſt Abhorrence of any the leaſt Fraud, and I could not help ſuſpecting that the Man, who had ſo long been uſed to miſtake Artifice for Openneſs of Heart, would, by the ſame Rule, miſinterpret Simplicity and Honeſty, for Perfidy and Cunning. But notwithſtanding all my

Fears, and the Terror I had of being again a Wife, after I had lost *Marcellus*; yet the Necessity I saw of my being made a Sacrifice to prevent the Effusion of Blood, which must be the certain Result of an intestine War, inspired me with a Resolution to overcome every Reluctance, in order to oblige my Brother, and prevailed on me to give my Hand to *Anthony* (I confess, indeed without my Heart). An Action the World should not have bribed me to have complied with, had I been born in private Life, and had not my relentless Fate obliged me so to do. We went together to *Rome*, to celebrate our Nuptials. We entered in Triumph, amidst the Acclamations of the People; who being harrassed and tired out with so many civil Wars, rejoiced in this Reconciliation between *Cæsar* and *Anthony*. That I was the Cause of this general Joy, and the Pledge of this Peace or Harmony, gave me also a Share in the Pleasure with which it inspired others; and, in a great measure, mitigated the Reluctance I had to this Marriage. As soon as I was married, I resolved to be as cautious in all my Deportment to make *Anthony* a good Wife, as if he had been the Object of my Choice. Nay, I was the more watchful over my Behaviour, as fearing the Want of that Affection I had indulged

for

for *Marcellus*, might tempt me to be careless of my Conduct to a Husband for whom I had not the same Inclination, and of which Duty now was to supply the Place. We lived some time at *Rome*; but as I saw there yet remained great Jealousies in the Hearts of my Brother and my Husband, I was much rejoiced, when the latter, taking me with him, left *Rome*, and went to *Athens*. I flattered myself the Distance from each other was the most likely Means of preserving a Peace between them. The *Athenians* omitted nothing in their Power to render my Stay with them agreeable to me and *Anthony*. Though at Intervals he fell into the licentious Pleasures he had been accustomed to whilst he lived with *Cleopatra*, yet did he now mix these Pleasures with so much Attention to Learning, and such a Delight in the Conversation of honest and ingenious Men, that I began to imagine Time would engage him to see the Folly of his profligate Manners; and as he had an extensive Understanding, and a good-natured Disposition, that he would be reclaimed from Vice, and act the Part most worthy of him.

Whether it was that I was a new Object, or that the present Object always made the strongest Impression on the Senses of the amorous *Anthony*, I could not determine;

determine; but he seemed now to have forgot *Cleopatra*, and to have fixed his Love on me alone. My Aversion to this Match did not arise from any Dislike to *Anthony*'s Person (for he was very agreeable), but from a general Dislike to being married again, and from some Objections to *Anthony*'s Character. However, now his kind Endeavours to oblige me, and his indulgent Behaviour, excited my Gratitude; which, added to the Duty I was sensible I owed my Husband, created in me an ardent and true Affection. But, alas! he was gone too far. Custom had too much blinded his Eyes, for him ever to be attentive to Truth; and from the Time my Affection was joined to my Duty, I began to lose Ground with him, and observed his Love to decrease. For *Anthony*, notwithstanding all the Affectation of an extravagant Passion, which his Wife and Mistress had deceived him with, was yet a Stranger to the living with a Woman whose Heart was open, and whose Love was disinterested and sincere. So much a Stranger was he to the very Marks of an unfeigned Passion, that not seeing those Storms of Rage he had been accustomed to with those to whom he had been the greatest Dupe, he could not fancy that Affection real, which wanted *such Marks*. He misrepresented to himself all my Actions, and disingenu-

ously interpreted all my Words. My never giving him an Hint about *Cleopatra* (for I was afraid to offend, and hated the very Thoughts of upbraiding him) he looked on as a Sign of Indifference. He had been used to so many Reproaches, that he knew not what to make of a Woman, whose constant Endeavour it was to keep up in his Mind agreeable Images, and to banish thence every Reflection which could shock or displease him. As he was very passionate, if those Men whom I knew to be his real Friends had inadvertently done any thing to provoke his Anger, I always endeavoured to conceal it; both as I was very unwilling he should rashly disoblige his Friends, and also because it deeply affected me to see him in those Agonies, which are usually caused by violent Passion. But if this was ever afterwards discovered, he looked on my attempting to conceal it as an Instance of Dissimulation. Whilst I was labouring to preserve his Friends, he thought me capable of siding with his Enemies. If any Scheme suggested itself to me, which I imagined for his Advantage, I immediately apprised him of it, without any Precaution; but this I found put him out of Humour, tho' I was then ignorant of the Reason of it. It seems *Cleopatra* had always brought about her own Purposes, by an artful Manner of making him believe
her

her Projects were originally his own. It entered not into my Head, that a Man of *Anthony*'s Understanding could live with a Woman as a Rival, and be angry with her, because her whole Mind, employed on him, sometimes proposed a Scheme for his Emolument, which had not happened first to come from himself. I had been used to live with *Marcellus* in so free and undisguised a Manner, that I had no Idea of concealing any lurking Suspicions within my Bosom which I should be ashamed of having avowed to the World; and as I had never once dreamed of any Superiority over my Husband, his supposing my harbouring such a Thought, was beyond my Comprehension. But yet, unfortunately for me, I had always the Reputation of having an Understanding uncommon for a Woman: And this Reputation made *Anthony* imagine that I valued myself on it, and presumed to be his Equal. Though far distant from me was any such Fancy, yet was he so satisfied of its Truth, that he sometimes, for a Week together, would treat me with a Surliness not at all like his natural Disposition; and the common Subject of his Discourse was, the Contempt he had for all Women of Sense. This would he accompany with such Looks, and speak in such a Voice, as plainly proved his Satire was levelled at *Octavia*. The

Observation,

Observation, that Satire does not hurt except the Cap fits us, may perhaps be true in our Commerce with Strangers; but where Affection is concerned, there is nothing more false. It is the Unkindness of the Person which levels the Satire at us, and not the Satire itself, that pierces the Soul. What then was it to me to live with the Man I loved, who was daily inventing new Ways, and various Expressions, to give me Torment? Small was the Relief which arose from the Consideration of my not deserving his Satire. For though his Words could not, yet the Unkindness of the Speaker wounded me to the Heart; and so unpardonable was this Fault of having an Understanding, that it made *Anthony* incapable of pitying my Infirmities, or commiserating my Sufferings. Alas! how melancholy was the Reflection that it was necessary for my Husband to entertain a Contempt for me, before it could be in my Power to raise his Compassion! I could not help fearing that Compassion so raised, took its Rise from some other Motive than mere Good-nature. To conquer Love, whilst we live with the Person we have long thought the Object of it, is probably as difficult a Task as can be allotted the human Mind: But when that Object is a Husband who claims our Duty, and has a Right to our Obedience, what is it but to tear away our Inclinations from the Object to whose Will and Pleasure we are obliged to submit? A Situation too dreadful to be described!

So little did I value myself on my Understanding, that I would willingly have parted with it, to have gained my Husband's Love. I saw the Cause of my Wretchedness, and at the same time was conscious how impossible it was to correct my Fault; for when once *Anthony* was convinced in himself that I imagined his Understanding was inferior to mine, all my Compliance with his Will, and Submission to his Judgment, appeared to him as so many Artifices to recommend my own. He supposed I submitted, as People sometimes do to Children, for the Sake of present Quiet, and not from a Conviction of his Superiority. However, *Anthony*'s Disposition was such, that at Intervals, this Whim being out of his Mind, his Love would revive, and then he was very willing to confess himself in the Wrong; and as soon as he took this Turn, he was uneasy till he was reconciled. The Moment I saw him uneasy, my own Eagerness to remove any the least Pain I but fancied he felt, incited me to be beforehand with him, and to exert the utmost in my Power to accomplish a Reconciliation. Thus, whenever he used me ill, I had

the

the Vexation of supporting that Treatment, whilst I also shared any Anxiety it might create my Husband afterwards. But this made him careless how often he quarrelled with, or, to speak more properly, how often he abused me; for that could not well be called a Quarrel, wherein I acted no Part, unless of Suffering. He would often give my Satisfaction at seeing him in good Temper again, so ill-natured a Construction as perfectly astonished me; for he insisted on its being a Proof how much better Women are for being sometimes treated with Severity and Rigour. My Affection would not permit me to behold him a Moment in any Grief, which it was in my Power to remove; and as the removing even the least Appearance of it was my Point in View, I never hesitated an Instant how I should behave. This Conduct erased from the Mind of *Anthony* all Fear in his Converse with me; and I was very sensible that an artful Woman (who in all Disputes had no Consideration for what he felt, but who employed her Thoughts in endeavouring to work some secret Purpose of her own, from the Hastiness of his Temper, and therefore, under the Pretence of passionate Grief for his ill Treatment of her, kept up the Dispute, and was reconciled just as she thought proper, to make him cautious in his future Behaviour to her) would have

have led *Anthony* to make another Discovery; namely, how necessary it is for a Man's own Happiness, to use the Woman with whom he lives, with Lenity and Good-nature. There is in every Mind some Degree of the Passion of Fear. Misfortunes I could support, and Death I could have met with more Resolution than the Frowns and Ill-humour of the Man I loved. To avoid this dreaded Evil was the chief Study of my Life; but I destroyed my own Purpose, and suffering my Apprehension of *Anthony*'s Displeasure to act too strongly, I overcame his Fears; and therefore when he was in an Ill-humour, he looked on me as the fittest Object to vent it upon. When I was first married to *Anthony*, my Submission to him arose from Duty; but when I loved him, I watched his very Looks, in order to execute his Commands even before he spoke them. Then by degrees, I lost him; and what most surprised me, were his repeated Complaints that I did not obey him. I examined myself continually, and still increased my Care, that he should have no Cause for these Complaints. But, Fool that I was! by this Management, instead of curing, I augmented the Evil.

I had

OCTAVIA. 205

I had been accuftomed to live with *Marcellus*, who loved me for my honeft Simplicity; and where Art was required to preferve a Man's Affections, it was impoffible but I muft lofe them. I was young, and very handfome; yet, notwithftanding all *Anthony*'s Admiration of Beauty, even that had not Force enough to prevent his making ufe of Artifices, which cannot be practifed by thofe who feel a true Love; for at once to be actuated by the violent Turns of Paffion, and coolly to follow the Dictates of a flow and lingering Burning, is beyond our Power. When we had lived at *Athens* this unhappy Life (for fo it was to me) Five Years, another Scene opened to my View. The Jealoufies between *Anthony* and *Cæfar*, which were only fmothered, and not extinguifhed, by my being made the Sacrifice to Peace, were always ready to re kindle; and my Hufband, provoked at fome Reports he heard of *Cæfar*, fet Sail with a great Fleet for *Italy*. He failed to the Port of *Brundufium*; but being there refufed Harbour, he made for *Tarentum*. Here I prevailed with him to fend me to my Brother, in hopes I might obtain a Peace. I met *Cæfar* in the Way, accompanied with his Friends *Agrippa* and *Mæcenas*. After mutual Expreffions of Kindnefs, I conjured him to confider, that the Eyes of the whole
World

World were turned on me, on account of my Connection with the Two most celebrated Persons in it, himself and *Anthony*; to one of whom I was the Sister, and to the other a Wife. If, said I, pernicious Counsels should take Place, and War shall be the Consequence, *Octavia* will be wretched without Redress; for on which Side soever Victory falls, I shall be a certain Loser. In short, by my Prayers and Tears, I so pacified and softened my Brother, that I had the Pleasure of once more seeing myself the Cause of Harmony between him and my Husband. They granted my Request, to assist each other in the Wars wherein they were engaged. They parted very good Friends; *Cæsar* going to make War with *Pompey*, for the Recovery of *Sicily*, and *Anthony* setting Sail for *Asia*. But in his Way, his old Disease returned. He sent for *Cleopatra*, and again fastened on himself her Chains. Perhaps he was displeased at my Manner of parting with him. For, notwithstanding the Perplexity his Behaviour often occasioned, yet I really loved him; and when I knew that the Necessity of Affairs, and both his Honour and Interest, required our present Separation, lest my Grief should give him Uneasiness, I strove, with the utmost Efforts of my Resolution to conceal it from him: And whatever Sorrow I felt, I suppressed

pressed or smothered it, till he was at a Distance not to be affected by it. My Care was needless; for it was not in my Power to vex or displease him. However, being ignorant of the true State of his Mind, I acted with as much Caution, from the bare Fancy that I might possibly hurt him, as if I had really been the Object of his Love. As soon as I could compose my Thoughts after his Departure, I employed myself wholly in the Care of his Children, as well of those he had by *Fulvia*, as my own. The unfortunate Children, who had lost their Mother, were the Objects of my Compassion; and the Love I bore their Father, extended to them, as his Offspring. Nor did the News I had heard of *Cleopatra*, abate my Care, or irritate my Revenge to gratify itself on their helpless Innocence. To confess the Truth, Revenge was not much in my Disposition; and I now experienced the Falsehood of the Assertion, that Love may be turned into Hatred, and that Hatred be heightened in Proportion to the Degree of the Love it succeeds. Love indeed, when it is only the Consequence of Pride gratified, will vanish as soon as that Pride is piqued; and will surrender up its Place to Aversion; which is the more natural and more general Consequence of unbounded Pride. But as Love was my predominant Passion, it was

built

built on the Gratification of no other; and therefore its Disappointment, whatever it made me suffer, did not burst out into Rage. This I am certain of, that I did not hate *Anthony*. For though from this Time forward he treated me with the utmost Scorn and Neglect, yet I could with Pleasure hear of his Prosperity, and was concerned at his Ruin; notwithstanding his mad Passion for *Cleopatra* was the Occasion of it. When I heard of his miserable Retreat from *Parthia* (though his Haste to return to *Egypt* was the Foundation of that Misery), yet was I shocked with the Account of the Hardships he had endured; and also pleased with the Goodness of his Behaviour towards his Followers, when he had brought them into that Distress. One Action in which I could find any Reason to approve and, praise him, gave me more Satisfaction, than if, from the same Passion he had for *Cleopatra*, he would have lain himself at my Feet, whilst he was ravaging and destroying the rest of Mankind. The Particulars of *Anthony*'s future Conduct came to my Knowlege only by the means of *Cæsar*. For as he was now overwhelmed in Fondness for *Cleopatra*, who, I was conscious, had no View on him but to promote her own ambitious Designs; I expected to hear nothing that would tend to his Honour, and would not suffer any

one

one to mention to me what tended to his Disgrace. Although he neglected me, yet he was still my Husband; and I thought it did not become me to hear him reviled or defamed. I prevailed with even *Cæsar*, when he related Matters of Fact, to soften his Expressions of *Anthony*, in Complaisance and Respect to his unhappy Wife. Matters of Fact I esteemed it necessary to know, that I might endeavour as much as possible to palliate my Brother's Rage, and avert from *Anthony* the dreadful Consequences which seemed to threaten him from his present unfortunate Situation. I looked on him as one under the Prevalence of a malignant Distemper, and would (had my Power equalled my Will) have preserved him from its dire Effects. But all my Endeavours for his Preservation proved fruitless. He had given a Loose to his unbridled Passions, and thrown off the Reins that should have curbed his wild Imagination. My Mind from henceforward, whilst *Anthony* lived, laboured under great Anxiety, and I was in continual Alarm for his Security and Protection. I could not help attempting all that was in my Power to rescue my Husband from Destruction; and therefore, before the civil War had blazed into an inextinguishable Flame, with *Cæsar*'s Permission, I went to seek *Anthony*, to make one last Effort to snatch him

him from his impending Fate. But at *Athens* I received, among others, the following Letter from him, signifying his Pleasure that I should wait for him there, and proceed no farther.

Anthony to Octavia.

"I am apprised of your Arrival at *Athens*; and
"your Intentions of proceeding farther, in order to
"meet me. The Purpose of your Expedition I
"shall not dilate upon; but whatever it is, let me
"acquaint you, that your Attendance or Company
"will at present be neither proper or agreeable. I
"must therefore insist on your waiting for me at
"*Athens*, till you hear more of my Pleasure; which
"I hope you will not fail to comply with.

"*Yours*,

"Anthony."

By this I saw plainly he was linked too fast in *Cleopatra*'s Chains, to leave the least remaining Hope of his ever shaking them off. Her Fear of losing him, called forth all her Artifice; and by the Pretence of dying for Love of him, she raised his Compassion, and confined it entirely to herself; whilst Tears of real Sorrow dropped unheeded from my Eyes. Tears which flowed from the double Source of his cruel Scorn, and his approaching Ruin. However, no harsh Word against him broke from my Lips; nor did I intermix any bitter Reproaches in the Letters I wrote him, to know how he would have the Presents I had brought him from my Brother disposed of, as will appear from the following.

OCTAVIA to ANTHONY.

"Agreeable to your Pleasure (which I am ever
"constant to observe) I wait at *Athens*, expecting
"your farther Directions. In the mean while, per-
"mit me, dear *Anthony*, to beg the Favour of con-
"sulting you in relation to the Disposal of the Pre-
"sents I have brought you from my Brother. Your
"Commands on this, and all other Occasions, shall
"be faithfully obeyed by her who, impatient of see-
"ing you, is, with all Sincerity,

"*Your affectionate and obedient Wife,*

"OCTAVIA."

But I soon received his Commands, in a contemptuous Epistle, to return to *Rome*.

ANTHONY to OCTAVIA.

" Your repeated Letters are troublesome and impertinent. The only Answer I shall vouchsafe them is, to command you to return immediately to *Rome*.

" *Yours,*

" ANTHONY."

I complied with his Orders; and now I expected the War could no longer be delayed: For *Cæsar*, I knew, would not brook this Indignity; nor could I in any shape soften it enough to conceal it from his penetrating Eyes. He insisted much that I should leave my Husband's House, and accept of an Apartment in his Palace. But I intreated him to let me continue where *Anthony* had placed me, unless I should receive from him Orders to remove. I thought at this critical Time to quit his House, would be making the Indignity more public, and increase the Clamour already too general at *Rome* against *Anthony*.

His

His Unkindness, how much soever I suffered by it, could not tempt me to be careless of his Honour. For, from the Instant I became his Wife, I determined, whatever might be his Conduct towards me, to make his Interest and Honour my chief Concern, and the Rule of my Actions. But vain was my Caution; for *Anthony* himself, infatuated by *Cleopatra*, soon sent proper Officers to remove me from his House; which I could not leave without Tears, at the Consideration, that although I had been made so great a Sacrifice for the Sake of Peace, I should now be deemed one of the principal Causes of a bloody War. I took with me all *Anthony*'s Children, except his eldest Son *Antyllus*, by *Fulvia*, who was with his Father. It was in vain for me longer to endeavour to mitigate *Cæsar*'s Wrath. He was deaf to my reiterated Prayers and Intreaties. And now approached the Event I had so much dreaded; when, after many Recriminations on both Sides, was let loose the Fury of a civil War, by which my Husband or my Brother was to be exterminated, and the Universe to obey only One Master. This produced the famous Battle of *Actium*, which (to humour *Cleopatra*) was fought by Sea, and in the midst of which she fled, and betrayed *Anthony*; who, to reward her treacherous Flight, left his Friends, and followed her as
a Captive.

a Captive. From this Moment she invented new Ways to betray him, and devised new Methods how she should abandon him to Misery, in order to make her Peace with *Cæsar*; till at last, by her Contrivance, his Fleet and Army surrendered themselves, before his Face, to the Conqueror's Mercy and Discretion. From the Time of this Battle, I had conveyed to him repeated Messages, to beg him, before it was too late, to preserve himself, and let me again be the Means of his being reconciled to *Cæsar:* But in the very Instant that he knew *Cleopatra* had betrayed him, on a Report of her being dead, he chose to kill himself for her sake, and by Self-murder to fly from *Octavia*, who was yet ready to receive him, and use her utmost Endeavours to crown him with Peace and Empire. Strange Infatuation! He had lived Five Years with me to very little Purpose, if he was still so ignorant of my Disposition, as to imagine I would once have hinted at any Reproach for his past Infidelity. I knew it was impossible to recall back Yesterday, and I would not have recalled back its Sorrows. To have been continually opening a Wound I was particularly desirous of healing, would have been the most effectual Method of destroying my own Design. But whatever Thoughts *Anthony*'s blind Passion for the ensnaring Queen of

Egypt

Egypt inspired him with, in prejudice of his unhappy Wife, yet did his Death alone put an End to my Solicitude for his Safety: And as to *Cleopatra*, no insolent Triumph over her once entered my Mind. It had always been my Maxim, that Vice brought its own Punishment; and I was not sorry that she escaped the Insults with which the enraged *Romans* were prepared to have treated her. The Sufferings of *Cleopatra* could not have recalled *Anthony* to Life, nor have restored him to *Octavia*; and I was capable of some Pity even towards a Rival. I omitted no Honour or Regard I could pay my Husband's Memory, although I did not affect any extravagant Grief for his Loss. Nay, I concealed what I really did feel; for I knew, that in a World where the slightest Provocations generally excite inveterate Hatred, it would have been thought incredible that I could derive any thing but Pleasure from the Misery or Death of a Man who had used me with Neglect and Scorn.

From this Time forward I proposed to lead a recluse and private Life, employed in the Protection of my own and *Anthony*'s Children. But, alas! my Train of Misfortunes was not yet compleated. For the young *Marcellus*, my Son by the best of Husbands

bands and of Men, was arrested and taken from me by the inexorable Summons of Fate. He was in the Flower of his Age; and had, as well by his filial Duty, as great Improvements, amply compensated my Care in the Education of him. His Virtues and Accomplishments had rendered him the Object both of private Esteem and public Admiration. *Cæsar* had entertained so high an Opinion of his Merit, as to chuse him for his Successor in the *Roman* Empire; and his Choice met with universal Approbation. My Brother, and the whole State, lamented his Death, and paid him every Honour that could consecrate his Memory, or demonstrate their unaffected Concern. But amongst all these public Expressions of Honour, none equalled the celebrated Eulogy of the Poet *Virgil*, which has so deservedly immortalized his own and the Character of my beloved Son. Neither the Emperor nor myself could refrain from Tears at the Recital of his pathetic Description; and when he mentioned the Name of my Son *Marcellus*, I fainted away; and thus gave Testimony both to the Power of the Poet, and the Intenseness of my own Affliction. To resist this unexpected Event, required the utmost Efforts of my Resolution. It struck to my Heart its pointed Arrow; and though I could stifle outward Complaints, yet I could not but feel

an

OCTAVIA.

an inward Anxiety So deeply was I affected, that I could never after bear to see any Picture or Image of him; nor suffer his Name to be mentioned, nor the Verses written in his Praise to be recited. My having been long accustomed to subdue my Passions, and keep them from insulting over my Reason, was indeed of inexpressible Service to me on this Occasion: It preserved me from exposing myself to Distraction by an Excess of Grief, and restrained within some Bounds my Sorrows, even for the Loss of this Pledge of Love left me by my Husband *Marcellus*. Nevertheless, so fatal an Accident gave a more serious Turn to my Mind than usual, and fixed a kind of Melancholy on me, which I could not even desire to cast off, as it now became my greatest Relief. This, however, did not prevent me from exerting myself to perform what I thought my Duty. In *Anthony*'s Life I had always taken care of his Children by *Fulvia*; but after his Death, I observed the Education, and considered the Fortune, of those Children brought him by the Queen of *Egypt*; and I married the young *Cleopatra* to the King of *Mauritania*, who was celebrated for his Knowlege of the Sciences, and the Strength of his Understanding. Revenge, as I have before said, had a very small Share in my Com-
position;

position; and I think, had I been naturally inclined to it, the Troubles which now diftreffed me muft have foftened my Refentment, and fuppreffed my Rage. I lived yet Thirteen Years, after the Lofs of my Son *Marcellus*; but I quitted the Court, and fpent my Time in Solitude and Retirement; where Books and Philofophy were both my Support and Amufement. From Reflection I had nothing to vex or upbraid me, in reference to my Behaviour. The Children, as well *Fulvia's* as my own, anfwered my Expectation, and I faw them happy around me. My Soul was clear as a limpid Stream. No Paffion difcompofed my Tranquility; and I became as unruffled by perplexing Sorrow, as a fmiling Infant. When I recollected my paft Life, I had the Pleafure of confidering, that notwithftanding the many unavoidable Misfortunes I had endured, yet, as I had acted uprightly, and without Guile, I could not condemn myfelf for being the Caufe of any of thofe Misfortunes. My honeft Simplicity, by procuring the Efteem and Love of *Marcellus*, was compenfated with more Happinefs than could have been my Fate by any bafe Defigns, or perfidious Treachery.

At

At length did I receive the Reward of conscious Virtue; for, applauded by the *Romans*, valued by their Emperor, gratefully treated by my Children, and with a Mind steady, serene, and calm, I sunk in Peace, and resigned my Breath, without any Remorse to embitter, or One Thought of Terror to disturb, my last and departing Moments.

F I N I S.